A DEADLY DAME

Liz wasted no time sliding through the cut in the rear of the tent. As soon as she stepped through, though, she heard something. Suddenly, an arm snaked around her neck, cutting off her air. She couldn't breathe.

"I thought I saw something, but I was not sure," a man said in Spanish. He must be the man who had entered the tent. "I had no idea I would find something so . . . pleasant." His other hand came around and closed over one of Liz's breasts. *"Qué linda!"* he said.

Liz could have reached her gun, but the sound of a shot would have brought the whole camp down on her. As the man slid his hand insider her shirt and squeezed her breast, laughing softly in her ear, she took out Sanchez's knife and stabbed backward, hoping that she would hit a vital spot.

Grunting in surprise as the knife bit into him, the bandit released her. She pulled the knife free quickly and turned and slashed at this throat before he could cry out.

ANGEL EYES

ANGEL EYES

#9

ANGEL FOR HIRE

Also by Robert J. Randisi

Angel Eyes

Tracker

Mountain Jack Pike

ANGEL EYES

#9

ANGEL FOR HIRE

Robert J. Randisi

SPEAKING VOLUMES, LLC
NAPLES, FLORIDA
2013

ANGEL EYES
#9 ANGEL FOR HIRE

ISBN 978-1-61232-591-0

PROLOGUE

Chris Tanner waved the pretty saloon girl over and asked her to bring him another *cerveza*. She gave him a flirtatious smile and went to get him a second beer. If he hadn't been there on business, he thought, watching her hips sway as she walked away . . .

But he was in Little Mesa, Mexico on business. He had been asked to meet someone there, although he didn't know who. What he did know was why. His business was fighting, and whoever was meeting him here had a fight that he couldn't handle, one he wanted to hire Chris Tanner to handle for him.

Tanner was thirty-eight and had been fighting for a living for most of his life. He was big and strong, fast with a gun, good with a knife, and he was smart. These qualities had combined to keep him alive in a business where most men died young. In fact, he had seen many men who had fought with him die before they were thirty, some of them friends of his.

He'd keep fighting for a living until he, too, was dead. It was the only way he knew how to live, and it was the way he would die.

The girl came back with the beer, and he admired the way her large breasts moved beneath her peasant blouse. She had good shoulders, wide enough to carry her big breasts proudly, and he knew she had good, strong legs.

Tanner didn't usually take women when he was working, but this was not a hard and fast rule with him. Every woman he had might be his last, and there were times when he found one that he just didn't want to pass up.

Like this one.

"What's your name, señorita?" he asked.

"Maria."

"Do you just work here, or does your father or brother own this *cantina*?"

"I work here," she said. "My father is dead, and I have no brothers."

"And no husband?"

She smiled and said, "No husband." Smiling revealed her only imperfection. She had two crooked teeth, one on either side of her two front teeth. Not crooked enough, however, to change his mind about her.

He was about to speak to her again when a man entered the small *cantina* and looked around the room. He had the helpless, anxious look that most of the men who hired Chris Tanner had.

"Perhaps we can talk later," he said to Maria.

She smiled and said, "Sí, señor, or perhaps we can do more than just talk."

As she walked away toward the bar, Tanner waited for the man to notice him before drinking his beer. When that happened, he held the man's eyes, and the Mexican finally decided to come over and ask.

"*Por favor*, señor, but are you Chris Tanner?" He pronounced it "Chrees."

"I'm Chris Tanner."

"My name is Pablo Mendez, señor. It is I who sent for you."

"Sit down," Tanner said. "Would you like a drink?"

"No, thank you, señor."

"Then you might as well tell me why you're here, Pablo Mendez."

"I have heard, señor, that you help those less fortunate —"

Tanner held his hand up to stop the man before he went any further.

"I am not a charitable man, Pablo. I don't help the less fortunate. I help whoever pays me. Do you have enough money?"

"We do not have very much, señor," Pablo said, "but we have some."

"You're going to have a hard time holding my interest with talk like that, Pablo."

"Please, señor. If I can tell you the whole story,

you will see that it will be to your great advantage to help me."

"Tell me the story, then."

"My town is called 'La Isla Bonita,' señor. Do you know what that means?"

"The Pretty Island?" Tanner said. "That's a hell of a name for a town."

"When you arrive, you will see why it is called that."

"Well, let's get to the point before we talk about my going there."

"Sí, the point, señor. Our town is being terrorized by a band of *bandido*s who want it for themselves. They want us to move out so they can move in. But señor, we built this town with our bare hands, my friends and myself. We do not intend to leave."

"You'd die before leaving?"

"If we must die we will die defending our homes . . . but we do not want to die, señor."

"So fight them."

"We have, señor, but we are no match."

"Why don't they just come down and take the town, then?"

"Along with the town they want our women. I believe they are afraid that if they attack us the women will be killed. And so, they wait."

"I see, so you want to hire me to come and fight them for you."

"Sí, señor."

"I'd need to bring some other men with me, Pablo. How would you pay us?"

"We have some money, but the *bandidos* have more," Pablo said. "They have a cave that is filled with many treasures. If you defeat them, what is theirs will become yours."

"What do you mean by treasures?"

"They have gold, and money, and other valuables. All that they have stolen is there."

"You've seen this?"

Pablo shook his head.

"But someone from my town has."

Tanner thought it over. If what Pablo was saying was true there might be more in this job than there had ever been in any of the others.

"How many bandits are we talking about, Pablo?"

"Thirty, perhaps forty," Pablo said. "You will need many men, señor. Perhaps fifty."

Sure, Tanner thought, split the treasure with fifty men and suddenly it wouldn't be worth much.

"I'll need less than that, Pablo."

"You will come, señor? You will save my town?"

"Yes, Pablo, I'll come."

"Then we must leave," Pablo said, abruptly standing up.

"Whoa. I've got to collect my men, first."

"How long will it take to collect so many men?"

"Not long. In fact, you can come with me. Where is your town?"

"Four days east of Mexico City."

That meant that Tanner could pick up men on the way. He knew of several fighting men who were in Mexico at the moment, and he could send telegraph messages to others in New Mexico and Texas. He felt fairly certain he could amass a force of fifteen or so, which would be plenty. The men he would use were worth any two or three Mexican bandits.

"When will we leave, señor Tanner?"

"In the morning, Pablo. You go over and stay at the hotel."

"I have no money for a hotel, señor."

"Here," Tanner said, taking his hotel room key from his pocket. "Stay in my room."

"But where will you stay, señor?"

Tanner looked at Maria, who was standing at the bar watching him.

"Don't worry about me, Pablo," he said. "I'll find someplace to stay."

Chris Tanner enjoyed the weight of the girl on top of him. She dangled her full breasts in his face and he caught her nipples in his mouth as she rode him up and down easily.

After Pablo had gone to his hotel, Tanner and the girl had gone to her room above the *cantina.* Their agreement to do so had been wordless. She had undressed for him, showing him her bare, brown skin, her full breasts with even darker brown nipples, her wide hips and strong thighs and the dark, wiry patch of hair between her legs. The first thing he did after he undressed was to bury his face in that patch of hair, and explore her with his tongue until she shuddered and screamed.

Later, she leaned over him, her hair covering his hips, and slid her mouth down over him. He lifted his buttocks off the bed as she suckled him, and then groaned aloud when he exploded into her hungry mouth.

Now she began to ride him a little faster, so that it was hard for him to keep her nipples in his mouth. Finally, she sat up on him and began to bounce up and down enthusiastically. Her large breasts bounced and jiggled, and he watched them in fascination until he felt that rush building up in his legs. It seemed to start at his heels and move up through his legs and thighs until it finally emptied out of him inside of her. She bit her lower lip as he spurted into her, and he watched the blood trickle down over her chin. Then she threw her head back and cried out as she came, too.

"You are leaving in the morning?" she asked.

"Yes," Tanner said, lying beside her, totally spent. He had never experienced a woman like her before. It disconcerted him that he did not want to leave.

"Will you come back?"

"I don't know, Maria."

"This job you will be doing, it is dangerous?"

"Yes."

"And you might die?"

"It's possible."

She put her head on his chest and he touched her hair.

"I will come with you," she said.

He opened his mouth to object, and was totally shocked when the word, "Yes," came from his mouth.

CHAPTER ONE

Liz Archer sat up in bed and stretched her arms over her head. The wound gave her a twinge of discomfort, but for the most part it was healed — at last! She'd felt like an invalid for so long.

She looked down at Tate Gilmore, sleeping next to her, and smiled. She and Tate had finally proclaimed their love for one another, after they had both nearly been killed in Mexico City. After several years of hit-and-miss sex, they had finally agreed that they belonged together.

They had come here to the home of Tate's friend, Matthew Callison, so that she could heal properly. Neither of them had wanted to remain in Mexico City any longer than they had to. It was not a place they looked back on with fondness, in spite of the fact that it was where they had finally come to terms with their feelings.

Callison had built his home on the beach, and Liz could hear the water outside the window. She rose carefully, so as not to wake Tate, and padded naked to the window to look out. She inhaled the sea breeze, thankful to be alive. She opened the window and closed her eyes as the breeze played over her naked breasts.

"What do you see out there?" Tate asked behind her.

She turned and looked at him. It had always amazed her how he could look wide awake immediately after waking.

"Just the ocean," she said. "It's beautiful."

"So are you."

She looked down at herself. To her own eyes she was less than beautiful. She had lost weight since being shot, and she could see her ribs outlined against her skin. She felt that even her full breasts had gotten smaller.

"I've lost too much weight."

"Hey," he said, smiling, "I like skinny women."

"Oh yeah? You never told me that before."

"You were never skinny before."

"Oh? And what was I? Fat?"

Tate grimaced. He had gotten caught in a trap. Never talk to a woman about her weight, or her age. Those were unwritten rules he tried to live by. Another rule of his was never to let a woman get to him, but he'd broken that rule the first time he'd

met Liz Archer, a young woman out for vengeance
with her father's Walker Colt in her hand.[1]

"Come here," he said, stretching out a hand to
her.

"Answer my question first."

"You were and are what you always will be," he
said, "beautiful."

She grinned and walked to the bed. He threw
back the sheet, revealing his own nakedness. Tall
and rangy, he was strong without being muscular,
which was just fine with her. She took a moment to
stare at his body, because she loved it. He opened
his arms, and she slid into his grasp.

He held her tightly, enjoying the way her flesh
felt against his. She was the warmest woman he'd
ever held. He experienced her for a few more
moments, then kissed her. It started as a tender kiss
and evolved into one of great passion. Liz moaned
deep in her throat as Tate's hands began to explore
her body. He touched her breasts, tweaked her
pink nipples, slid his hands down the curve of her
back to cup her smooth buttocks, and then pulled
her down on top of him.

Liz smiled as she felt his erection trapped between them. She knew that this time it was going to
be quick and powerful. Later, they'd make love
more tenderly.

She placed her hands against his chest, raised her
hips and slid his full length into her, slamming her
loins against his, swallowing him in one great gulp.

1. ANGEL EYES #1

She felt his hands on her buttocks, lifting her, sliding her up and down the length of him. She closed her eyes and threw her head back, moving her hips.

Soon the room was filled with the sound of their flesh slapping together faster and faster as their passion mounted. She was moaning when she finally came, and then she jammed herself down tightly against him. Moments later she felt him filling her, and without meaning to, Liz scratched his chest as she came again.

"I'm sorry about this," she said later, touching the three bloody lines on his chest.

"That's all right," he told her, taking her hand. "These are the kind of scars I don't mind carrying."

He had other scars, many of them caused by knives and bullets. By his own count he had been shot seven times, and attributed his survival to luck and the will to live.

"How could I have died any of those times?" he asked. "Then I wouldn't have met you, would I?"

"You mean, somehow you knew we'd meet?"

He smiled and said, "I don't know if my meaning was that deep."

"That's a scary thought," she said. "That would mean that it was prearranged that we would meet, by some higher intelligence."

"Like God?" he asked.

"Yes, like God."

He chucked her under the chin and said, "This conversation is getting out of hand. Let's go downstairs and see if we can't get Consuelo to fix us a big breakfast. I'm starved, and you need to put on some weight."

"See!" she said, slapping his ass as he hopped off the bed. "You don't like skinny women!"

CHAPTER TWO

Once downstairs they found they didn't have to try to convince Consuelo to make them a large breakfast. She had already done so.

"Consuelo," Tate said, "this is magnificent."

"*Grácias*, señor," Consuelo said, lowering her head shyly. She was Callison's housekeeper, although Liz suspected that she was much more than that and had mentioned it to Tate one night while they were in bed.

"That's silly," Tate had said.

"Is it? She's an attractive woman."

"She's a very handsome woman," Tate had agreed, "but Matt is . . . is . . ."

"Sixty years old?" Liz asked. "So what? That doesn't mean he can't enjoy a woman anymore — and Consuelo is only in her forties."

"What makes you think they're lovers?"

"The way she looks at him."

"Why don't you sneak over to his room one night and see if they're together."

"I will," she said, "if you'll sneak over to hers. If they're doing it, one of us will catch them."

"And embarrass them."

They waited a moment, and then Liz said, "Why don't we just go on wondering?"

"That's just what I was going to say."

Consuelo had laid out a huge American breakfast of eggs, ham, potatoes, biscuits, flapjacks with maple syrup, and coffee.

Liz and Tate had just seated themselves when Matt Callison entered.

Liz wished she could have seen Callison twenty years ago, or even ten. Even now he was a tall, broad-shouldered man with the handsome face of an aristocrat. In fact, he was of German descent and had hinted more than once at some royalty in his blood. He sported a full head of flowing white hair that reminded Liz of a lion she had once seen in a circus. He also had a full and well cared for mustache and beard.

"Good morning," he said, his voice booming. "Ah, I thought I smelled one of Consuelo's masterpieces. This is in your honor, I'll have you know."

"As has every meal been since we've arrived, according to you," Liz told him. "Doesn't she feed you well when you're alone, Matt?"

Callison laughed and said, "Not this well."

He was fit and trim and if not for the white hair would have looked ten years younger. There did not appear to be an ounce of fat on him, so apparently Consuelo fed him just the right amount of food.

"Come on, now, dig in," he urged. "We don't want to insult Consuelo."

By the time they were finished Consuelo definitely had no reason to feel insulted. They had all done her spread justice, especially Liz, whose appetite had been returning these past few days.

"Keep eating like that, Elizabeth, and you'll be filled out in no time — although I must say, you look extremely pretty just the way you are."

"Why, thank you, Matt." She liked the way he insisted on using her full name because it was — in his words — much too beautiful to be shortened.

She lifted her chin and said to Tate, "Some men know how to talk to a lady."

"Now you've gone and done it, Matt," Tate said. "She'll be expecting me to compliment her all the time, now."

"And so she should expect it," Callison said. To Liz he added, "If he does any less, you let me know at once."

"I will."

Consuelo cleared the table and brought out a second pot of coffee. After she had poured them each a cup and left, Callison turned serious and took out an envelope.

"This came for you, Tate."

"Mail?" Tate said, frowning. "When could that have come?"

"This morning," Callison said. "I have my own little postal service."

"But who would know I was here?"

"We've had some guests since you arrived. Word could have gotten around."

Callison was right. He was one of the finest gunsmiths Tate had ever known, and many men — some gunmen, some not — sought him out to have their weapons worked on. Some of the men who had arrived during Tate and Liz's stay had been acquaintances of Tate's, and others had simply recognized him. He realized that Callison was right. Word could have gotten around very easily.

"What is it?" Liz asked.

Tate read the note, which was short and to the point. He handed it to Liz, and then turned to Callison.

"Somebody wants me to meet them in a *cantina* in Mexico City."

"Who?"

"The note doesn't say."

"Why, then?"

"According to the note, it could mean a lot of money."

"Is that enough of a reason to respond to an unsigned note?" Callison asked.

"No," Tate said, "but curiosity might be." He turned to Liz and said, "What do you think? Are you fit to ride?"

"Sure I am," she said, handing him back the note. "Besides, I think we've imposed enough on Matt and Consuelo."

"Elizabeth, having you here has been no imposition," Callison said, putting his hand over hers, "and I know Consuelo feels the same. She's enjoyed having another woman around for a while.''

"Still, it's about time we got moving, Matt,'' Tate announced. "We can't stay here forever.''

"You could,'' Callison said, "but I know what you mean, Tate.''

"We'll pack our gear and leave this morning. The note sets the meeting for the same time every evening for the next week.''

"And after that?'' Callison asked.

Tate shrugged.

"I guess after that the meeting is off.''

"What if it's some kind of trap?'' Callison asked.

"I don't think the present regime has any reason to want me dead,'' Tate said, rising from the table. "Besides, I'll have very competent backup.''

"Ooh,'' Liz said playfully, "the compliments are starting already, aren't they?''

By the time Tate and Liz came downstairs with their gear, their host had their horses saddled.

"You're both welcome back here any time,'' Callison said, handing them their reins.

"We know that, Matt,'' Tate said. He extended his hand and Callison took it, shaking it firmly.

He turned to Liz and said, "Come back some time without him.''

"I just might do that,'' she told him and hugged him tightly. Surprised, he hesitated before hugging her in return.

"Consuelo?'' Liz said. The dark-haired woman stepped from the house and the two women embraced.

"Vaya con díos," Consuelo whispered.

A look passed between them that Tate wondered about, but he didn't bring it up just then. They mounted, waved and rode away.

They followed the beach for a few miles before turning inward and heading for Mexico City.

CHAPTER THREE

Pete Sanchez threw down two cards, lovingly fondling the three nines still in his hands. He watched as the dealer fed him two more cards, and then turned to the next player to make a similar exchange. The man held a cigar in his hand while he dealt, and took a puff between players.

Sanchez picked up his two new cards and found a pair of sevens to go with the three nines. A beautiful full house. For a man who had been losing steadily all night, this was a hand sent from heaven.

He watched the other five players as they examined their hands. The man on his right had been the first to open. Sanchez had raised with his three nines, and to his delight everyone had stayed in. Sanchez did not subscribe to the theory that said you had a better chance of winning with fewer players in the game. He felt that a player dropping out was simply someone whose money he could not take.

"It's up to you," the dealer said to the opener. The dealer was American, and all of the other players were Mexican. The other Mexicans were residents of the town, Santa Madera, while Sanchez — like the gringo — was only passing through. It was the gringo who was the big winner.

"I am aware of that, señor," the opener said. "I bet five dollars." They were close enough to the border that the game was being played in American money.

"Fifteen," Sanchez said.

The player to his left snorted and folded his cards. The next man called the fifteen dollars.

It was up to the dealer.

"Make it twenty-five," he said.

The gringo had drawn one card, but even if he had made a straight or a flush, Sanchez knew he still had him with his full house.

The opener glared at the gringo and said, "I make it fifty." Clearly he was tired of losing to the Americano.

"While we are at it," Sanchez said, "why don't we just make it a hundred?"

Now the opener glared at Sanchez. His look seemed to accuse Sanchez of being a traitor, but Sanchez was playing for himself, not for Mexico against America. He simply smiled at the other man.

The fourth player in the game dropped out, and the gringo smiled across the table at Sanchez.

"Got a good hand, eh?"

Sanchez smiled.

"If I do, señor, it is the first one tonight."

The gringo laughed at that.

"How much money do you have left on the table?"

Sanchez looked down, counted, and replied, "Twenty-three dollars, señor."

"Then I raise twenty-three dollars."

The opener was getting angry. Both the American and Sanchez were acting as if he were not there.

"Aiie!" he said in disgust. "I piss on your raise, señor. Twenty-three dollars," he said, throwing the money in. But despite his annoyance he did not raise.

"Call," Sanchez said. "I have nines full, señor."

"Ah!" the opener said angrily. He threw his cards down, revealing his two pair, kings over fours.

"You did get a good hand," the gringo admitted. "Unfortunately, not good enough." He put his cigar between his teeth and laid down his cards. He too had a full house, only he had queens over threes.

"Your luck is unbelievable," Sanchez said, shaking his head.

"Do I take it you think it's more than luck?" the man asked while raking in his pot.

"If I thought that, señor," Sanchez said, rising, "you would be dead. *Grácias* for the game."

"Anytime."

Sanchez walked to the bar, where a chunky girl named Estralita was waiting.

"Have you lost all your money?" she asked sadly.

"Every peso, Lita."

"But you still have me, eh?" she asked.

Sanchez smiled. His even, white teeth added greatly to his dark, good looks which invariably made women fall into his arms — and his bed.

He put his arm around Lita and closed his hand over one of her muscular buttocks. Sanchez loved full-bodied women, and Estralita certainly fit that description. She had tits like cannonballs, and Sanchez was looking forward to burying his face between them.

"That's right, Lita. I still have you."

"You go to your hotel, I will join you shortly."

"Uh," he said, "a drink before I go?"

She leaned forward and whispered, "They do not give free drinks here. I will bring a bottle with me."

He kissed her soundly and said, "Don't make me wait too long. I am not as young as I once was, and I might fall asleep."

She pressed her impressive chest against him and said, "No, you will not. You will be waiting for me."

He laughed, slapped her buttock and left the *cantina*.

When he reached his hotel the desk clerk caught his attention and waved him over.

"A telegraph message for you, señor," the man said.

"When did it arrive?"

"Earlier, before dark, but I did not know where you were."

And you didn't bother to look, did you? Sanchez thought.

"Grácias," he said, taking the message and moving towards the stairs. He deliberately did not tip the clerk. The dog didn't deserve it.

In his room he read the message and found that it was from Chris Tanner. He had worked with Tanner many times, and it had always meant money. Unfortunately, it had always meant death, too. On one occasion they had started with twelve men, and finished with just the two of them still alive. Of course, they'd only had to split the proceeds in half, but it was depressing, nevertheless.

Tanner wanted Sanchez to meet him in a town called St. Tomas, which was south of Santa Madera.

Sanchez folded the message and put it in his shirt pocket, then took off his shirt, readying himself for Estralita. This would have to be a memorable night, for he would be leaving Santa Madera much sooner than he had thought.

CHAPTER FOUR

Oren Brand ordered a whiskey and felt the eyes of everyone in the saloon on him. They were wondering if he was going to go out into the street and meet Dee Keller, or if he was going to use the back door to get away.

Robak, Texas had seen its share of showdowns in the street. In the past few months many of them had involved Dee Keller, a local product who fancied himself a fast man with a gun. So far, he had proven his claims correct on four different occasions.

Brand finished the drink and set it down, then called the bartender over. In his late forties, Brand was solidly built with muscular arms and large hands. He looked more like a wrestler than a gunman. In point of fact, he did not consider himself a gunman in the way Tate Gilmore and Pete Sanchez were gunmen. Oren Brand didn't have their slender hands or their speed. He was steady though, and accurate. He'd killed many men who had missed their first shot because they were trying too hard for speed. They never got a second chance.

The bartender came over and was about to ask him what he wanted when Brand took hold of the man by the throat.

"You sent this punk a message, didn't you?" he demanded. "Huh?" He shook the man by the throat.

"I don't —" the bartender started to say, but Brand squeezed the man's reply off. It would have been a lie, anyway.

"You're his scout, right? You see a likely looking gent in here and you send him word, right? He shows up and picks a fight. He's your town gunny, right?"

The man, red in the face, nodded.

Brand released him and the bartender slumped against the bar, breathing raggedly.

"When I come back in here, friend, you better be gone."

"Wha —"

"Your friend will be dead by then, and if you're still here, you will be, too. Understand?"

Now pale with terror, the man nodded.

Oren Brand turned and walked outside.

Keller was fast, all right, but he couldn't hit the side of a barn from inside. Brand put a bullet in the boy's chest after Keller had gotten off a shot, which went wide.

He wondered how many times Keller had fired in the past before hitting his man.

As Brand walked away the clerk from the telegraph office stepped into the street.

"For you, Mr. Brand."

"When did you get this?"

" 'bout half hour ago."

"Why didn't you give it to me, then?"

"Didn't think you'd be needing it," the man said. "Guess I was wrong."

"You sure were," Brand said, giving the man a flat, hard stare.

The clerk swallowed nervously and muttered, "I . . . I got to get back."

Brand quickly read the message. It was from Chris Tanner. He'd never worked with Tanner, but he'd heard of him.

It looked like it was time for them to meet.

When the knock sounded on the door Reggie Northrop had his face buried between Cherry McClain's legs. Cherry was a nineteen-year-old redhead who happened to be the mayor's daughter. It had taken them a lot of sneaking around to get to this point.

Reggie ignored the knock until it became insistant.

"What is it?" he demanded, coming up for air.

"Ooh, Reggie, don't stop," Cherry moaned, reaching for his head. "I'm almost there!"

"Telegraph message for you, Mr. Northrop."

"Jesus —" Northrop said in disgust. "Slip it under the door!"

"But —"

It was the desk clerk, who was obviously worried about getting a tip.

"You want a tip, damn it?" Northrop shouted.

Not shy, the clerk said, "Well, it is customary."

"Well, slide that damned thing under the door and get lost. That's the best tip I can give you, friend," Northrop shouted. Cherry managed to get her fingers tangled in his hair and was pulling his face back into her wet warmth. "It'll do your health good!" he added just before he went back to munching on Cherry.

Later, after Cherry had climaxed, her screams muffled by a pillow, she watched as Northrop walked over and picked the piece of paper off the floor.

"God, you're a beautiful man!" she said in awe.

"Well, you're a beautiful woman, Cherry," he said. "You deserve the best."

"Conceited, too!"

He spread his arms and executed a small bow.

"Have I got something to be conceited about?"

"And how!"

"I rest my case."

While he was reading the message she said, "I have to get back, you know. My father will have my brothers looking for me."

"You've got brothers?" he asked. That was news to him.

"Two of them. Big brutes."

"How big?"

"Real big."

"Uh-huh," he said, reading the message again.

It was from Chris Tanner, with whom Northrop had ridden several times. He wanted Northrop to meet him in a town called St. Tomas, within the next week and a half.

"Two brothers, huh?" he said again.

"Two," she agreed, nodding. "And a husband."

"A husband?" he asked in disbelief. "Now why didn't you tell me that before?"

She shrugged, making her big breasts jiggle. "You never asked."

She was right. He never had. In fact, he never *ever* asked, which was why he'd often had to leave the arms of women in a hurry.

Not this time, though. She might have brothers and a husband, but they weren't pounding on the door.

Not yet, anyway.

"You want me to leave?" she asked.

"I thought you said you had to."

"I didn't mean right *now*!"

He put Tanner's message on the dresser and returned to the warmth of the bed, and of Cherry's skin . . . and mouth.

"I still have some time . . ." he said.

CHAPTER FIVE

Chris Tanner had sent out twelve messages, asking eleven of the recipients to meet him in St. Tomas. He was reasonably sure that he would see Sanchez and Northrop, because they'd worked together before, and worked well. Both men were dependable and good with a gun. The only problem would be that they'd be trying to *look* better than each other. They were both real ladies' men. For a moment Tanner wondered how Maria would react to them, but he quickly pushed that thought from his mind.

Tate Gilmore was the only one he'd asked to meet him in Mexico City. Part of the reason for that was that Maria had never been to Mexico City, and Tanner wanted to take her there.

The other reason was that he wanted to talk to Gilmore before he saw the rest of them. He felt that the success of this particular job depended on recruiting Gilmore — which wouldn't be easy.

Tanner and Maria had spent the day — their fourth — walking around Mexico City. Maria never got tired of walking, just as she never seemed to get tired of sex.

They were in bed, and Maria was busy between his legs. Her educated mouth was bringing him to a stiffness he had never known before, and each time it seemed like he was going to explode, she did something to keep him from doing so. She prolonged it for so long that when he finally did come it was almost painful, and he was ejaculating so much that he doubted that she'd be able to handle it.

But, of course, she did.

Each time they had sex, she impressed him more. Not only was she tireless, but she managed to keep him going, as well.

"This is a magnificent city," she said moments later as they lay side by side.

"Wait," he told her, running his finger around and around one of her nipples. "Wait until we have money, Maria. I'll show you cities that make this seem like a village."

"Truly, Chris?" she asked, still pronouncing it "Chrees." He liked it when she said his name like that.

"Truly."

"You are very generous to me," she said, kissing him deeply.

"I haven't even begun," he murmured, turning

towards her so he could bury his face between her breasts.

Later, after they made love again, he lay in bed staring at the ceiling.

He was afraid.

He'd never felt anything this strong for a woman before. It seemed to be having an effect on him. He wasn't the same man anymore.

He was starting to hope that the return on this job would be so large that he wouldn't ever have to do this kind of work again.

CHAPTER SIX

When Tate and Liz approached Mexico City they stopped just outside the city limits.

"We can call this off, you know," Tate said to her.

Liz shuddered, and took a deep breath before answering.

"There's no need."

"I mean, if you don't want to go —"

"Tate, let's go."

"We might have to wait around for him to arrive."

"Or her," Liz said.

"Her?"

"Maybe it's an old girlfriend," she said, teasing him. "Did you ever think of that?"

"No, I never did. Come on."

After they entered Mexico City they purposely

picked a hotel far from the Presidential Palace. They didn't want to run into anyone.

In their room Liz walked to the window and Tate came up behind her.

"What do you think it's about?" she asked him.

"I don't know."

"What if it is a trap, like Callison said?"

"I doubt it."

"Why?"

"Because I can smell something like that."

"Tate —"

He turned her around and kissed her, then hugged her to him.

"I'll go in first, you stay outside and watch."

"But —"

"The reason I don't think it's a trap is because I got the message at Matt's place. Somebody setting a trap for me wouldn't know about Matt's."

"You mean the message has to be from a friend?"

"Not a friend, necessarily, but from someone who knows me, someone I probably know, and someone who knows about Matt's operation. Believe me, that's no one in the Mexican army."

"They don't know about Matt?"

"No."

"How can he operate in their country without them knowing about him? Doesn't he supply guns to rebels, or —"

"Matt's a gunsmith. He's been known to sell guns, but only to regular customers — and his regular customers don't talk to anyone. This is not a trap, Liz. Don't worry about that."

She put her arms around his waist and pressed her head to his chest.

Did he really believe that, or was he just trying to put her at ease, Liz wondered.

She felt his heart beating quickly, but she chose to believe that was because he loved her.

"When should we go to the *cantina*?" she asked.

"After dark."

"Where is it?"

"Not far from here."

"Any chance that we'll run into anyone . . . accidentally?"

He laughed.

"Not in that part of the city. No one from the Palace would even slum there."

He held her at arm's length and said, "We'd better get some rest, huh?"

"You mean in bed?"

"Where else would I mean?"

"Together?"

"We only have one bed."

"In bed, together, and you want to rest?" she asked.

"Well," he said, unbuttoning her shirt, "maybe just a little."

CHAPTER SEVEN

It was after dark when Liz and Tate left their hotel to head for the *cantina* and their mysterious meeting.

"We still have time to forget about this," Liz said.

"Why should we?"

"I'm worried."

"Well, I'm curious."

"Tate —"

"Let's just do it the way we planned, Liz. Okay?"

She stiffened, not liking his tone. He realized it and stopped walking.

"I'm sorry, Liz," Tate said, taking her by the shoulders gently. "I didn't mean to make that sound like — well, I'm sorry. I'm not trying to *tell* you what to do. If you don't want to go —"

"That's not it," she said. "If you go, I go, I'm just not sure either of us should go."

He stared at her for a few moments, then said, "We're quite a pair, aren't we?"

"What do you mean?"

"We're both stubborn, both have minds of our own. I guess we're going to do our share of head butting."

"It wouldn't be interesting if we didn't, would it?" she asked.

He laughed and said, "I guess not."

They stood like that for a few moments, and then Liz said, "Well, are we going, or aren't we?"

"We're going, we're going," he said, and they started toward the *cantina*.

Chris Tanner told Maria Alonso that she couldn't go with him.

"Why not?"

"It's not a very good section of the city."

"I would be with you."

"I don't want to have to worry about you, Maria."

"This man you are meeting, he is dangerous?"

"Very dangerous."

"Is he your friend?"

Tanner hesitated, then said, "Not exactly. The fact of the matter is, he might not be so glad to see me."

"He will try to kill you?"

"No," he said. "This man is possibly the best hand I've ever seen with a gun, but he won't try to kill me. He doesn't like to kill."

"I will worry," she said, kneeling on the bed. Her little girl pout and the proud thrust of her large breasts were in sharp contrast to each other, but together they made her even more desirable.

He moved to the bed, took her face in his hands and kissed her more tenderly than he'd ever kissed another woman. The rush of emotion he felt for her still frightened him.

"I want you to worry," he said. "I'll be back soon."

When he left she sat back on the bed and shook her head. He was the most interesting, most frustrating, most stubborn man she'd ever been with.

Tanner arrived first and positioned himself in a doorway across the street from the *cantina*. It wouldn't be wise to go inside if Gilmore wasn't going to show up. In that kind of place, you could get in trouble without blinking an eye, and he didn't need any trouble just now.

He'd been there an hour when he saw Gilmore coming down the street with a blonde woman. From what he could see she was young, well-built, and was wearing a gun.

He'd heard about a blonde gunwoman, but had never put much credence in the story.

He wondered . . .

Tate and Liz stopped outside the *cantina*.

"I wonder if he's in there?"

"I don't think so," Tate said, looking around. "But he's here."

"How do you know? Where?"

"Don't turn around," he said. "There's someone standing in a doorway across the street."

"Maybe it's just a drunk."

"This is no drunk. When I go inside you keep
walking. Go a block and double back and watch
that doorway. Wait for him to move first, Liz.
Don't get impatient, no matter how long it takes."

"All right."

"Go ahead, now."

Tate entered the *cantina* and Liz did as he said.
She walked a block, crossed over and used the
shadows to hide her progress back. She reached a
point where she could see the *cantina* entrance,
stepped into a doorway herself, and waited.

Tanner saw Gilmore enter the *cantina*, but the
woman continued down the street. He followed her
progress but in less than twenty yards she was
swallowed up by the darkness.

If he was Gilmore and had brought backup, he
would have told her to double back. He could have
waited to see if she'd move first, but he decided not
to play that game. He wasn't there to do Gilmore
any harm, he was there to make him some money.

He'd never heard of Tate Gilmore hiring out
before, but as he stepped from the doorway and
started across the street, he hoped to change his
mind.

CHAPTER EIGHT

As soon as Chris Tanner walked in, Tate Gilmore knew he'd made a mistake in coming. His curiosity had gotten the better of him, and now he was going to have to deal with Tanner, a man he disliked intensely.

He waited while Tanner looked around the crowded room. Tate had been lucky to find a table after getting his beer from the bartender. He'd only been sitting there fifteen minutes, but had already turned away the advances of two Mexican whores.

Now he was going to have to turn away the advances of an American whore.

Tanner spotted him finally. You couldn't tell by his expression, but Tate saw his eyes, and knew. Tanner took the time to walk to the bar and order a beer, then carried it to Tate's table.

"Is this seat taken?" he asked.

"I'm not receiving any whores tonight, Tanner."

Tanner shook his head and smiled slightly. There was a time when a remark like that would have angered him, but he needed Tate Gilmore.

He sat down.

"I'm gonna ignore that remark for now, Tate. I've got a proposition for you."

Tate stared at Tanner in surprise. The man had a notorious temper, and he had just purposely tried to anger him to get him to leave. He didn't like men who sold their guns for money, and that meant he didn't like Tanner. In fact, he disliked Tanner even more than most hired guns because Tanner *recruited* other gunfighters. Tanner not only sold his own gun, but other people's as well.

"I've got a job —" Tanner began.

"Not interested."

"You know, Tate, you always were the most holier-than-thou killer I ever met."

Tate stiffened.

"I'm going to ignore that comment, Tanner — that is, providing you get up and leave now."

"I heard you had a bad time here in Mexico City a while back."

"It worked out."

"Make any money?"

"That's not —"

"No, you didn't make any money. Have you ever made any money, Tate? I mean, real money?"

"I get by."

"A man with your talent shouldn't just get by, Tate. Somebody who handles a gun like you should be rolling in money."

"Yeah," Tate said sarcastically, "I can see that you're rolling in money."

"Well, I take that as a compliment."

"I've never denied your talent, Chris," Tate said, using the other man's first name for the first time.

"Well, you're right about one thing," Tanner said. "I'm not rolling in money. Fact is, I spend it about as fast as I make it, but this job I got —"

"Not interested."

"— coming up, it's gonna take me some time to spend what I make, here."

"And you want to share it with me."

"Yup."

"Why?"

"Because I need you."

"You need my gun."

"Same thing. You are your gun, Tate, whether you want to admit it or not. I admitted that about myself a long time ago, and I've been better off for it."

"That's debatable."

"Look, I'm only asking you to listen to my offer," Tanner said. "Hell, you came to this meeting without even knowing who you were meeting with."

"If I had known I wouldn't have come."

"Ah, but you did. Your curiosity brought you, and your curiosity will make you listen to what I have to say."

Tate knew then he should get up and walk out, but he *had* ridden all this way.

"All right," he said finally, "talk."

Tanner talked. He told Tate what the job was, and told him about the bandits' treasure cache.

"Stolen, all of it," Tate said when Tanner was done.

"But who from? Who would we return it to, and if we can't return it are we supposed to just let it lie there?"

Tate didn't answer right away.

"You got a partner these days, Tate?"

"What do you mean?"

"I mean the blonde woman outside. Why don't you have her come in? It ain't safe for a lady out there."

With a start Tate realized that he had forgotten about Liz. He didn't see her at the door, but he knew she must be looking through the window.

He waved to her to come in.

Liz had been wondering what all the talking was about and was relieved when she saw Tate wave to her. She'd already had to turn away the amorous advances of two drunks.

Going inside, she got herself a beer and walked to Tate's table. She was well aware of the fact that her progress was closely watched by most of the men in the room. Even as thin as she was, she attracted men the way honey attracted flies.

When she reached the table both men stood up.

"Chris Tanner," Tate said, making the introductions, "Liz Archer."

"Liz Archer," Tanner said, eyeing her with obvious pleasure. Suddenly, though, he frowned and said her name in a different tone. "Liz Archer? Aren't you the one they call 'Angel Eyes'?"

"I suppose so," she said, seating herself. The two men also sat, Tanner still staring at her.

"I thought —" Tanner started.

"What did you think?" Liz asked.

"I thought you were a . . . a myth."

She sipped her beer and said, "I don't think I've quite reached mythic proportions, yet."

"Let's just say I thought you were the figment of someone's imagination."

"I'm real."

"I'll say you're real." Tanner looked at Tate and said, "Is she your partner, Tate? There's room for her, you know."

"Room for me where?"

Tate didn't reply, so Tanner said, "I've just made Tate an offer that could make him a lot of money — and you, as well. He'll tell you about it." Tanner finished his beer and put the empty mug on the table. "Meet me here tomorrow night, if you're interested." He looked at Liz and said, "Both of you, or either one."

As the gunman stood up, Tate said, "Chris."

"Yeah?"

"You didn't tell me why you need me. You've never tried to recruit me before."

Tanner turned to face Tate and hesitated a moment before speaking.

"This just might be my last one, Tate," he said. "The one I retire off of, and I want to come out of it alive. With you along my chances of doing that double . . . at least."

"You have a lot of faith in me."

"I've seen you in action." Tanner looked at Liz and said, "I haven't seen you in action, but I'm looking forward to it."

They watched as Tanner left, and then Liz turned to Tate and said, "What's the story?"

He told her.

CHAPTER NINE

After Tate had related Chris Tanner's proposal to Liz they decided to go back to their hotel to discuss it. They took a bottle of whiskey with them and worked on it diligently while they talked.

"There's another way to look at this, Tate," Liz said.

"What way is that?"

"Neither one of us has ever gotten anything but grief from our talents with a gun."

"That's true."

"Maybe it's time we did."

"How do you mean?"

"Maybe it's time we went ahead and let our guns make us some money."

"You mean kill for money?"

Liz hesitated. Beginning to feel drunk, she said very carefully, "If that's what it takes."

"I can't believe —"

"Who are we talking about, here?" she asked, interrupting him. "Some bandits who are terrorizing a town. Men who are probably killers themselves."

"You're trying to —"

"I'm trying to make you see that just this once it's all right to hire out. Tate, if we don't do it, what *will* we do? Take odd jobs? Me as a waitress, you as a ranch hand?"

"I've worked as a ranch hand before."

"And did it suit you?"

"No."

He took a swig from the bottle and found that he had emptied it.

"No more whiskey," he muttered.

"We don't need any more," she said, moving closer to him on the bed. "I think we're drunk enough to make our decision. All we have to do is stick by it when we're sober."

"You want to do this?" he asked. "You really want to do this?"

"Yes," she answered without hesitation.

He grimaced.

"I hate making this exception when Chris Tanner is involved, but if you really want to, then we will."

"Do you mean it?"

He smiled at her and said, "Yes."

"I wouldn't do it without you, you know. Not unless we both agreed to it."

"Well, I agree."

"I mean, you really don't have to if you don't —"

"Now that you've talked me into it, Liz, are you trying to talk me out of it?"

She grinned drunkenly and said, "No, I'm not. Let's go to bed."

"I'm too drunk."

She looked at him in surprise and said, "Too drunk to go to bed?"

He stared at her and then said, "Do you mean go to bed . . . or go to *bed*."

"I mean," she said, pushing him off the bed and onto the floor so she could pull the bed clothes down, "go to sleep!"

"That," he said, getting up off the floor, "I can do."

"Did he come tonight?" Maria asked when Tanner returned to their hotel.

"He came."

"And did you talk to him?"

"Yes?"

"And?"

He pulled off his boots and dropped them to the floor.

"He's thinking it over," he said. "We'll meet again tomorrow night for their decision."

"*Their* decision?"

Tanner nodded.

"He has a woman with him."

"And you want to hire her as well?"

"This is no ordinary woman," Tanner said. "They call her Angel Eyes."

"I have never heard of her. Is she pretty?"

"Very," he said, then looked at her and said, "but you have nothing to worry about, Maria."

"I will make sure I have nothing to worry about," she said, pushing him down on the bed and unbuttoning his shirt. "I will make sure that you have all the woman you can handle."

CHAPTER TEN

The following night Liz and Tate returned to the same *cantina*. This time they entered together. As soon as they settled down at a table, Tate smelled trouble.

"You see those men at the bar?" he asked.

"The three who have been watching us since we entered?"

"Yes."

"They're with the other three who are sitting at the table by the window," she said.

"Yes," Tate said, "so they are."

"Maybe all they'll do is look," Liz said hopefully.

"I don't know," Tate said. "That's what they did last night. But tonight they seem even more interested."

"I guess we'll just have to wait and see."

About twenty minutes later Chris Tanner walked in. He stopped at the bar for a beer and then joined them.

"Have you decided?" he asked without preamble.

"Yes," Tate said.

"We'll do it," Liz said.

Tanner looked surprised.

"You know," he said, looking at Tate, "I didn't think you would."

"I didn't think so, either," Tate admitted, sipping his beer glumly.

"When do we leave?" Liz asked.

"First light," Tanner said. "We'll be in St. Tomas in two days."

"And from there?"

"From there we go to a town called *La Isla Bonita*, 'The Pretty Island.' "

"Odd name for a town," Liz said.

"I thought so, too. Perhaps when we get there and see it, it won't be so odd."

"Who else is in on this little job?" Tate asked.

"We won't know that until we reach St Tomas," Tanner said. "I think we can count on Pete Sanchez and Reggie Northrop."

"If we can keep them away from mirrors, and women," Tate said.

"I see you know both of them."

"I know Reggie," Tate said, "I've heard of Pete. Who else have you contacted?"

"Oren Brand, Sam Marshal, Vernon Law, half a dozen others."

"Law's in jail," Tate said.

Tanner frowned.

"When did that happen?"

"A few months back. A dispute over a poker game."

"Shit. Well, there are still the others."

"How many bandits are we talking about, Chris?" Tate asked.

"My source tells me about thirty or forty."

"And who is your source?"

"Fella from the town named Mendez. I guess he's the unofficial mayor, or something. He'll be meeting us in St. Tomas, also."

"Anyone else we should know about?"

For a moment Tanner wondered if Tate had followed him last night and knew about Maria. Probably not, but he decided to go ahead and tell them about her, anyway.

"I've got a woman with me," Tanner said. "She'll be coming along."

"Can she handle a gun?"

"No," Tanner said, "but she can cook real good."

"Well, that's important," Liz said.

Tanner finished his beer and said, "I guess I'll turn in. We can meet at the end of Consuelo Street, at the northern edge of the city. First light, all right?"

"That's fine with us, but there's one thing we have to do first."

"What's that?" Tanner asked, frowning.

"We've got to get by them," Tate said, nodding his head. Tanner looked behind him and saw what Tate meant. The three men who had been seated by the window were now standing in front of the door. The three at the bar had straightened up and were staring at them.

"I think," Tate said, "they might want to borrow some money."

CHAPTER ELEVEN

"This would be easier," Tanner said, "if they were standing four and two."

Tate knew what he meant. If two of them faced the three men by the door, then the other would have to face the second group of three alone.

"I'll take the ones by the bar," Tate said.

Tanner agreed. He knew that Tate was better with a gun than he was, better — as he had told Maria — than anyone he ever knew — with the exception of Hickok, and even that was an arguable point.

Liz, however, did not agree so readily.

"Why should you take three on your own?" she asked.

"Why not?" Tate asked.

"I could take three."

"Liz —"

"Or don't you think I could?"

"Could we save this for another time?" Tanner asked. "Why don't you two at least stand up."

"You think these fellas understand English, Chris?"

"I don't know," Tanner said. "I'll ask them." He turned and said, "Do you understand English?"

No reply.

"Spikka de English?"

No reply.

"Habla ingles?"

"Money," one of the men by the bar said, and the other people in the *cantina* reacted by dropping to the floor or running for the back of the room. In seconds the only thing in the room besides the six Mexicans and the three Americans was an expanse of floor covered with overturned tables and chairs.

"Maybe we should stand up," Liz said.

"In a minute," Tate said. "I'm going to stand, you stay seated. It might keep them off guard."

Slowly, Tate stood, holding his hands out in front of him.

"No money," he said to them.

No reply.

"No dinero."

Still, no reply.

"Señors," the spokesman by the bar said, "put all your valuables on the table, and you may leave."

"Who are you kidding, friend?" Tate said. "You aren't going to let us leave."

"Wait a minute, Tate," Tanner said, "let's not be hasty. Maybe they do intend to let us live."

"Maybe, " Tate said, "but I don't want to wait to find out."

With that Tate reached across the table and grabbed Tanner. At the same time, he gripped the edge of the table with his other hand. For an instant Tanner thought Tate was going to use him as a shield, but then Tate pulled him across the table, flipped the table over to use as cover, and drew his gun.

As soon as Liz saw Tate move she reached for her gun and threw herself sideways.

Tate was the first to fire, with Liz a close second. Before the Mexicans even drew their guns two of their number were dead.

From the floor, where he lay sprawled after being pulled over the table, Chris Tanner drew and fired by instinct, and felled a third Mexican.

By now the other three had drawn their guns, but before they could even aim, Tate, Liz and Tanner fired together, leaving all six Mexicans dead on the floor. Next to three of them lay their guns. The other three still had their weapons in their holsters.

"Let's get out of here," Tate said, "before a crowd gathers."

"Good idea," Tanner agreed, picking himself up off the floor.

All three of them holstered their guns and left the *cantina*, stepping over the bodies of their would-be robbers, and killers.

Once they were far enough away from the *cantina* and fairly sure they were out of danger they stopped in an alley and took the time to reload.

"All right," Tate said, "we'll meet you at first light as planned."

"Do you have good horses?" Tanner asked.

"We do," Tate said.

"Then don't be late."

"Why?" Tate asked. "You going to leave without us?"

When Liz and Tate reached their hotel they removed their gunbelts and hung them on a bed post.

"What do you think about what happened at the *cantina*?" Liz asked.

"What do you mean?"

"Was it a coincidence? Were those men there just to rob us, or to kill us to keep us from going with Tanner?"

"I think your mind is just a little too devious, Liz," Tate said. "Tanner is recruiting us to deal with some bandits. I don't think that any *bandidos* are going to be so worried about us that they'd send half a dozen men to Mexico City to kill us — and Tanner."

"Then it was a coincidence?"

"We were in a real bad part of the city, you know."

"So it was a coincidence."

Tate made a face. Liz knew how much he hated the word "coincidence."

"All right," he finally said, "so when we leave the city we'll be extra alert. All right?"

She grinned, nodded and said, "All right."

"Now let's take care of something very important before we go to sleep," Tate said.

"Are we going to make love?"

"No," Tate said, "we're going to clean our guns."

"Is it done?" Maria asked when Tanner entered the room.

"It's done," he said, removing his gunbelt. "We'll meet at first light and be on our way to St. Tomas."

"Santo," she said to him, "I keep telling you it is Santo Tomas."

"Sure," he said, sitting on the bed and sliding his gun from its holster.

"Are you coming to bed?" she asked, pressing her cheek to his back.

"Soon," he said, "after I clean my gun."

"There was trouble?"

"Some," he said, "but nothing like there's gonna be."

CHAPTER TWELVE

Hector Enrique Montalvo looked down at the town of *La Isla Bonita* and thought again about storming it and taking it from its residents.

And again he rejected the thought.

The town was self-sufficient. The people there grew their own vegetables, bred their own meat, and obtained water from a nearby stream. Much of the work was done by the women, he knew.

As the leader of the *bandidos*, Montalvo wanted the town for his new headquarters, but he wanted the women as well, to make sure that the town continued to run efficiently. If he was going to launch a successful revolution, the first thing he needed was a proper headquarters.

And this was it.

"We should go down and take it away from them," said his second-in-command, Jaime Santana.

"Have you been reading my mind, Jaime?" Montalvo asked.

"Then that is what we will do, Hector?" Santana asked hopefully.

"No, Jaime," Montalvo said, "that is what we will not do."

"But why?"

"I have told you why."

"Yes, the women," Jaime said. "Hector, we can get many women. I know women who would be proud to come and serve the new revolution."

"I do not want just any women," Montalvo said, "I want those women."

"But why?"

"Because they know how to keep the town running," Montalvo said, "and because they are beautiful."

"You are thinking only of one woman, Hector, and she has bewitched you since the first time you saw her."

Montalvo could not deny it, so he did not offer an answer. He knew that he was bewitched by Katarina Mendez, but he was not so enamored of her that he would throw away his revolution for her.

He wanted her to be part of it.

"Has there been any sign of Mendez yet?" he asked Santana.

"Not yet. Do you think he has run off?"

"No, not him," Montalvo said. "He has probably gone for help."

"What kind of help could he get?" Santana demanded. "Who could he afford?"

"No one who could be any danger to us."

"Hector, will you come back to camp now?" Santana asked.

"Soon, Jaime," Montalvo said, "soon."

Santana watched his leader for a few moments, then shook his head and went back to camp.

Katarina Mendez saw Hector Montalvo up on the ridge, watching the town — watching her!

She wondered when her father would return.

Sometimes, during the days since he had gone, she had found herself wondering *if* he would return.

At first light Tate and Liz arrived at the appointed meeting place and found Tanner and a woman waiting for them. They both noticed that the woman was extremely handsome and full figured.

"Good morning, Tanner," Tate said.

"Tate, Miss Archer."

"If we're going to be travelling together," Liz said, "I think you should call me Liz."

"All right, Liz. This is Maria. She will be coming with us."

"Hello, Maria," Liz said.

Maria nodded to both Liz and Tate.

"Shall we go? It will take us a couple of days to reach St. Tomas."

CHAPTER THIRTEEN

The ride to St. Tomas was uneventful, to the relief of all concerned. Even Tanner had been wondering if what had happened at the *cantina* that night had been more than a coincidence. Since nothing had happened during the trip, and they apparently hadn't been followed, Liz and Tanner were ready to admit that the six Mexicans had been after no more than their money.

Grudgingly, Tate had to agree — almost.

When they reached St. Tomas Tate and Liz found it was an extremely small town. In fact, it was hardly a town at all. It looked more like a stage stop. There was a hotel, a *cantina*, and a livery stable, and not much else. It seemed that at one time there had been more buildings, but they had all either fallen down, been burned, or just wasted away.

"Not much of a town," Tate grumbled.

"It serves a purpose," Tanner said.

"You've used this before?"

"Many times. We'll leave the horses at the livery and go over to the hotel. I hope the others haven't been too crowded there. There aren't that many rooms."

They took their horses to the livery, where Tanner talked to a wizened old man he called Tito. Tanner took the horses inside with Tito while the others waited outside.

"Strange," Tanner said when he returned.

"What is?" Liz asked.

"There are only four horses inside. I was sure there'd be more."

"Maybe everyone hasn't arrived yet." Liz suggested.

"That's probably it," Tanner agreed.

They went to the hotel, where they were very easily able to get two rooms.

"The others will have to sleep in the livery, I guess," Tanner said. "It'll only be for one night, I hope."

"I hope so too," Tate said.

"Where are the others?"

"Others?" the clerk asked.

"Where could they be, Tanner?" Tate asked. "We've been to the livery and the hotel."

Tanner thought for a moment. "Let's get over to the saloon."

They left the hotel and went to the *cantina*. When they walked in they saw three men sitting at a table playing stud poker, and a bored bartender dozing with his elbows on the bar.

It only took Tate a second to realize Reggie Northrop was one of the card players.

Tanner recognized Northrop and Sanchez immediately. He assumed that the other man was Oren Brand.

Liz saw two very good-looking men in their mid-thirties, one American and one Mexican. The third man, not nearly as attractive, was American, stockily built, and in his late forties.

"Three men?" Tate asked.

"There were four horses in the livery," Liz said, reminding them.

"The fourth one must belong to Mendez."

"Your friend Mendez is asleep at the hotel," Pete Sanchez said, recognizing Tanner and standing up.

"We were just playing some poker to while away the time," Northrop said, "and hoping that you had more men than this coming."

"I do," Tanner said. "At least, I thought I did. I contacted over twelve men."

Northrop and Sanchez walked over and began to eye both Maria and Liz appreciatively.

"Are you gonna introduce us?" Northrop asked.

"You know Gilmore, don't you?" Tanner asked.

"How are you, Tate?" Northrop said, but he was looking at Maria. Northrop was obviously attracted to the dark skin and hair of the beautiful Mexican woman.

Sanchez, on the other hand, looked to be much

more attracted by Liz's fair skin and blonde hair, and seemed especially taken by her blue eyes.

"Been a while, Reggie."

"A couple of years, I guess."

"This is Maria, Liz Archer, and Tate Gilmore," Tanner said. "Pete Sanchez."

"Pleased to meet you," Sanchez said, looking directly at Liz.

"Am I included in this gathering?" the third man at the table said.

"Oren Brand, right?" Tate said.

"Right. How'd you know?"

"You fit the description."

Brand and Tate shook hands and then Brand nodded shyly at the ladies.

"What's going on?" Brand asked.

"I appreciate you responding to my message, Brand," Tanner said.

"Just call me Oren, and is this it? Five guns?"

"Six," Tanner said, pointing to Liz's gun.

Brand looked at Liz's gun, then looked at her again and recognition dawned.

"You're Angel Eyes, aren't you?"

"I've been called that."

"Angel Eyes?" Northrop said, moving his gaze away from Maria reluctantly. "I thought that was —"

"A myth?" Liz said.

"Yeah."

"She hasn't reached mythic proportions, yet," Tanner said. "Look, let's sit down and I'll explain as much as I can."

They went to the table where Northrop, Sanchez

and Brand had been playing poker and cleared the table of the cards. Brand shuffled the deck while Tanner spoke.

When Tanner was done Northrop said, "How long do we give the others before we move on?"

"Wait a minute," Brand said. "Move on? You mean you're willing to go along with this with just the six of us?"

"Sure, why not? Listen, what's a few *bandidos* to us? I know all of your reputations, and I'm no slouch, either. We can handle it."

Everyone was silent for a moment, and then Tanner said, "What do you all say?"

"I'm in," Brand said.

Looking at Maria, Northrop said, "Why not?"

"Liz?"

Liz glanced at Tate, who nodded, and she said, "Count me in."

"That mean you too, Tate?"

"Yep."

His eyes on Liz, Sanchez said, "I guess that makes all of us."

"All right, then," Tanner said. "We'll move out at first light. If any of the others show up before we leave, so much the better."

Tanner stood and Maria did the same.

"We're going over to the hotel to get some rest, and I want to see Mendez."

"So do I," Tate said. "I'll come along."

"Me, too," Liz said.

"Can't you stay?" Sanchez asked her, smiling. Northrop was directing a similar toothy smile Maria's way.

"Got to freshen up," Liz said. "You boys continue your game. We'll see you later."

"For dinner," Tate said.

As Liz, Tate, Tanner and Maria left the *cantina* Liz said, "Promise me you won't ever leave me alone with him."

"Which one?" Tate asked.

"Either of them."

"I think Sanchez likes blonde *gringas*."

"As if I didn't have enough trouble."

CHAPTER FOURTEEN

"Why don't you ladies go ahead and freshen up?" Tate said when they arrived at the hotel. "We'll check on Mendez."

Liz was about to argue when she saw the look in Tate's eyes.

"Right, Maria, why don't we?"

"Very well. I will see you later," she said to Tanner.

"Sure, Maria."

Liz led the Mexican woman away, and Tanner knocked on Mendez's door.

"What's with the woman, Chris?"

"What do you mean?"

"I've never known you to travel with a woman."

Tanner looked down the hall, in the direction the women had gone, and said, "Maybe that's part of the reason why I want this to be my last job."

"I see."

"What about you?" Tanner said, knocking again. "I've never known you to travel with a woman."

"Yeah, well, things change, don't they?" Tate asked.

"They sure do."

Tanner knocked again, then looked at Tate.

"Why isn't he answering?" he said.

"Maybe he can't," Tate said.

Tanner turned the doorknob and found the door unlocked. He drew his gun and opened the door. They both saw Mendez lying on the bed, looking dead to the world.

Liz and Maria went down to the clerk to find out about taking a bath. He told them he had only one tub, but that he'd be glad to fill it for them and they could take turns.

Liz and Maria exchanged glances and Liz said, "Let's take it. Half a bath is better than none."

"Yes."

They waited while the clerk hurriedly filled a battered, scarred metal tub that looked as if it would begin to leak any minute.

After the clerk left they both undressed, each without a hint of shyness.

When they were naked they rather unashamedly examined one another.

Even if Liz hadn't lost weight because of her injury Maria would have been heavier than she was. Both had full breasts, but where Liz's hips and legs were slender, Maria's were plump. She had an earthy, sensual quality to her that Liz knew would appeal to men.

"You have been injured recently," Maria said.

"Yes. I've lost weight."

"You are very beautiful," Maria admitted.

"Thank you."

"Your skin, and your eyes," Maria said, "your body . . . if I were a man — or a different kind of woman — I would find you very desirable."

"You're very lovely, as well."

"I am not so beautiful as you, but I am satisfied. Would you like to go first?"

"No, that's all right," Liz told her, "go ahead."

"If it was a little larger," Maria said, "there would be room for both of us."

Liz thought there was a hint of regret in Maria's voice. Liz had been with another woman only once in her life, a Chinese girl in San Francisco[1] and while she had found the experience very pleasurable, it was not one she was looking to repeat. She much preferred men, and Tate in particular.

She wondered about Maria's past experiences. The darker woman kept glancing at her with what seemed like more than impersonal detachment.

Tate found the empty whiskey bottle on the floor.

"He's dead, all right," he said, picking it up, "dead drunk."

Tanner put his gun away and slapped Mendez's face a couple of times.

"He's really out," he said. "We can dump some

1. ANGEL EYES #4: CHINATOWN JUSTICE.

cold water on him, or wait until he wakes up on his own.''

''Let's wait,'' Tate said.

As they moved to the door Tanner said, ''I hope he's fit to travel tomorrow.''

''If he isn't, we'll just toss him over a horse and take him along.''

As the two women bathed, they talked, got to know each other, and even discussed their men. When they were done with their bath they dressed and walked upstairs together.

''I think we will get along very nicely,'' Maria said to Liz in the hall outside their rooms.

''I think so too, Maria.''

Their rooms were opposite each other, and they said good night as they opened their doors and entered.

CHAPTER FIFTEEN

"Tired?" Liz asked Tate.

They were in bed, naked, her breasts pressed firmly against his back.

"Never too tired for you," Tate said, turning into her arms.

They kissed, her hand snaking between them and taking hold of him. She rubbed her nipples against the hair on his chest as his hands slid down her back to clutch at her buttocks. He rolled over onto his back, taking her with him, and then she lifted her hips so that he could slide into her easily, fully.

Later she said, "Are we doing the right thing?"

"It's too late to ask that now," he said.

"But six of us . . ."

"I've faced lousier odds."

"How often?"

He smiled in the darkness, held her closer and said, "Once."

Tanner lay still — or tried to — while Maria worked her magic between his legs. Her tongue fluttered along the length of him, her mouth closed over him, drawing on him, until he could no longer hold back.

"Is this madness?" she asked when they were done.

"Us together? Hardly."

"I mean six guns, against many."

"That," he said, "might be called madness, yes."

"Then why do it?"

"The rewards will be great," he said, "but maybe . . ."

"Maybe what?"

"Maybe you should stay behind."

"Here? And do what?"

"It's too dangerous —"

"I am coming with you, Chris," she said. "Please, no argument."

He held her close and said, "All right. We'll go together."

Tate and Tanner were back at Mendez's door the next morning. Again it was unlocked, and they walked in. It was as if he hadn't moved. The bottle was still there, the stench was still there, the man was still there, only he was no longer dead drunk.

He was simply dead.

"How?" Liz asked.

"His throat was cut while he slept," Tate said.

She and Tate were in their hotel room with Tanner and Maria.

"What does this mean?" Maria demanded. "Why would someone kill him?"

"We don't know, Maria," Tate said.

"What are we going to do, then?" Liz asked.

"We'll go on," Tanner said. "We'll do what we were hired to do. Mendez mentioned a daughter to me. When we get to *La Isla Bonita*, we'll talk to her."

"What about the others?" Liz asked. "Do we tell them?"

Tate and Tanner exchanged glances.

"Nothing," Tate finally said, and Tanner nodded.

They met Sanchez, Northrop and Brand at the livery, all saddled and ready to go.

"You're late," Northrop complained.

"Overslept," Tate said.

Tate and Tanner went inside and saddled all four horses. When they came walking out with the mounts Brand asked the question they were waiting for.

"Where's Mendez?"

"We'll see Mendez," Tanner said, "when we get there."

They moved out, seven riders on their way to a town with a pretty name — where what was waiting for them was not pretty at all.

Reggie Northrop said under his breath, "Tate Gilmore never overslept a day in his life."

Katarina Mendez awoke that morning with a start. She looked around her room, wondering what it was that had woken her, what it was that was giving her such a chill. She rose, pulled a robe around herself and walked to the window. Most of the buildings in *La Isla* were of one floor only, as was the two room house her father had built for them. She had a bedroom, but her father usually slept on a pallet in the other room, which served as a living room and a dining room.

She went out into the other room, walked to the front door and opened it. The sun was coming up and she pulled the robe tightly around her against the cool morning air.

The sun was coming up for her, she thought, but not for her father.

She felt with a cold certainty that he was dead.

What would become of them now?

CHAPTER SIXTEEN

It was a four-day ride to *La Isla*, and Mendez's absence seemed to weigh heavily on everyone until finally, the last night on the trail, Northrop brought it up.

"If we're going to work together on this I think we should be honest with each other," he said over coffee.

"Have you a confession to make, Northrop?" Sanchez asked, reluctantly turning away from Liz to look at Northrop.

"No, but someone does," Northrop said. "What happened to Mendez?" he demanded.

Tanner looked at Tate, who nodded, and then at Liz, who also nodded.

"He's dead."

"Dead?" Brand asked. "When?"

"That last night in St. Tomas," Tanner said.

"How?" Sanchez asked.

"Somebody slit his throat while he was sleeping."

Brand looked behind him suddenly.

"Has anyone noticed someone on our tail?" he asked.

They all shook their heads.

"Could a killing like that be a coincidence?" Brand asked.

"I, for one, don't believe in coincidence," Tate said.

"Who could have killed him?" Sanchez asked.

"Anyone," Tate said. "Any one of us, for instance."

"Or someone from this town we're going to," Brand said. "The question is, why?"

"Maybe they figured that if the man who hired us was dead, we'd forget the whole thing," Northrop said.

"Could they be that scared of five —" Northrop started to say, then stopped himself, smiled at Liz and said, "excuse me, of six guns?"

"These six guns, maybe," Sanchez said.

"Should we set a watch?" Brand asked.

"Good idea," Tate agreed. He, Liz and Tanner had in fact been taking turns each night on an unofficial watch. Now that they were less than a day out of *La Isla*, a more official one was preferable.

"Let the ladies sleep," Sanchez said. "We can take one hour watches."

"Agreed."

Liz didn't argue, and Maria certainly did not.

They set the watches — Sanchez, Northrop, Tanner, Brand and Tate — and turned in.

When Brand woke Tate for his watch, Tate opened his eyes instantly.

"Anything?" he asked.

"Nothing I can put my finger on," Brand said. "I've kept the coffee pot going."

"I'll have a cup."

"I'll have one with you."

Over coffee Tate said, "What did you mean by nothing you could put your finger on?"

"I just have this feeling that we're being watched."

"Have you had it all along?"

"No, and that has me worried. That was why I asked if anyone had noticed anything. No, I think it's just tonight, now that we're close to town."

"You may be right."

"We're approaching this town from the south," Brand said. "Do we know where the *bandido* camp is?"

"The north, I think. I'd have to check with Tanner, but I don't think he'd have us coming in from the south if that's where their camp was."

"You a full partner on this, Tate?" Brand asked.

Tate shook his head.

"Just a hired hand."

"Do we really have six guns on this?"

"Are you asking me if Liz lives up to her reputation?"

"That's what I'm asking you."

"I'd put her up against any one of us."

"That's quite a statement."

"She's quite a woman."

"I can see that much," Brand said. "I'll take your word for the rest."

He poured the remains of his coffee onto the fire, causing it to flare up. Then he said, "I'll see you in about an hour or so."

"We'll get started at first light."

"Keep your eyes and ears open. Somebody might want to keep us from reaching town at all."

As Brand rolled himself up in his blanket, Tate looked around at all the sleeping forms. Could one of them be the killer, and if so, why? It didn't make sense. He thought it might even be someone from *La Isla*. Perhaps the bandits had put someone on Mendez's trail, to see who he was hiring, and then killed him to dissuade them.

If that was the case, there was a very good chance that they'd be attacked before reaching town.

But how many men would they face, he wondered.

Tate woke them all when the slightest tip of sun showed in the east. Each had his own way of waking, rolling out, stumbling out. Like him, Tanner awoke instantly. Liz took a little longer. Northrop and Sanchez were immediately concerned with their appearance, while Brand was concerned with his weapon and how *it* had survived the dampness of the night.

Tate had a full pot of coffee ready and they each had a cup before moving on.

Before they moved out, however, Tate recounted to the others the conversation he and Brand had had less than two hours earlier.

"I think he's right," Tanner admitted. "I felt the same thing, although I didn't see anything."

"All right, I have a suggestion," Tate said, looking to Tanner for approval. He did not want to usurp Tanner's authority, and the other man nodded his approval.

"I think we should avoid bunching up and ride spread out," he said. "That way if we are attacked they can't get us all at once."

"Makes sense," Tanner said. He looked at the others and they all nodded.

"How far are we from town?" Tate asked Tanner.

"From what Mendez told me, I'd say a few hours, at least."

"All right, I guess we'd better get moving."

"How do we convince the townspeople we're for them, and not against them?" Northrop asked. "They might not take too kindly to us riding in."

"I'll have to talk to Mendez's daughter and convince her," Tanner said. "If for some reason they do attack us, let's try to defend ourselves without killing anyone. After all, these are the people we came here to help. Any questions?"

No one offered any.

"Then let's ride."

CHAPTER SEVENTEEN

Tanner rode in front with Maria. Trailing along behind them were Brand and Northrop. Next came Tate and Liz, with Sanchez bringing up the rear.

They had been riding just over an hour when Sanchez called out, "Here they come."

They all looked back and saw a group of about a dozen men riding down on them from a ridge.

"All right, let's pick it up," Tanner cried. "Let's see if we can stay ahead of them."

They kicked their horses to life and began to ride them hard.

Tate's gelding was the superior horse, and Liz's mare was next. They began to pass the others, and Tate knew that the rest of the horses were tired from the days of travelling. Soon they'd be staggering, and the *bandidos* would catch up.

When he and Liz caught up to Tanner he

shouted, "We'll have to stop somewhere and make a stand! The horses can't keep up this pace."

Tanner nodded and called out, "You go ahead. Circle around."

Tate knew what he meant, and he and Liz continued to push their horses, putting some distance between themselves and the others.

When they were far enough ahead Tate waved at Liz, telling her to change direction. They were approaching a ravine that would be a perfect place for the others to make their stand.

They rode to some thick brush and took refuge behind it.

"We're not going to stand here and watch," Liz said.

"No. The bandits will have to assume that we got away when the others stopped to fight. When that happens, we'll come up from behind them."

"Six against twelve?"

"Considering what we've been expecting, two to one ain't bad odds," he said grimly. "We beat them in Mexico City."

She smiled and nodded.

"Besides, any kind of a crossfire gives an advantage."

They watched as Tanner and the others reached the ravine, pulled their horses up and dismounted. They let the horses go on and drew their guns.

As the *bandidos* passed them, Tate and Liz reined their horses around and rode out from the brush. Tanner and the others began to fire, while Tate and Liz came at the band from their right, also firing.

Like puppets on strings, the bandits began to be

jerked from their horses by chunks of hot lead. Before they could react to what was happening there were only four left, and they wheeled around and fled.

Tate and Liz approached the ravine and the others came out, smiling.

"That wasn't half bad," Tanner said.

"Serves notice, anyway," Northrop muttered.

"The next time they come for us," Sanchez said, "they'll bring more men."

That sobered everyone fairly quickly.

"Liz and I will gather your horses up. Anyone hurt?"

"No." Tanner looked around. "We came through unscathed."

"Good," Tate said. "Let's get those horses and be on our way."

"That must be it," Tanner announced.

"It doesn't look very pretty," Liz said.

"To them it might," Tate said.

"I see gardens," Maria said.

"And animals," Brand added. "Cows, goats, chickens — everything they need to be self-sufficient."

"And maybe that's what makes it pretty to them," Sanchez suggested.

"Makes it attractive to a band of bandits, also," Tate observed.

"As long as they know how to use what it offers," Tanner said. "That's why they haven't just stormed the place. They want to take it intact."

"If they're operating under that restriction,"

Tate mused, "it might give us an advantage."

"However slight," Liz said.

"Well," Tanner said, "let's ride on in and find out. I could do with a good meal."

Katarina responded to the insistent knocking on her door. It was her friend Juanita.

"What is it, Juanita?"

"Riders approaching."

"Montalvo's men?"

"No."

"How many riders?"

"Seven. Five men, two women."

"My father?"

"He is not with them."

"From what direction?"

"South."

Katarina nodded. She took an old Henry repeater from the wall where it hung and said, "Get the men up on the rooftops. I will meet them."

CHAPTER EIGHTEEN

As they approached the town they saw a woman standing in their path, holding a rifle. On the roof-tops they could just make out the tops of men's heads.

"That must be Mendez's daughter," Tanner said.

She's beautiful, Tate thought. He looked at the other men and knew they were thinking the same thing. He looked at Liz, who smiled and wiggled her eyebrows. He'd never known a woman before who was so self-assured that she never felt threatened by other women.

They approached the armed woman and stopped.

"You must be Katarina," Tanner said.

"How do you know my name?"

"Your father told me."

"You know my father?"

"He came to me, and my friends," Tanner said, indicating the others, "for help."

"Where is he?"

"May we take care of our horses, and get something to eat —"

"Where is my father?" she said, making a menacing gesture with the rifle.

Liz looked around but could still see no more than the heads of the men on the rooftops. None of them had moved so much as an inch.

"If we could talk inside —"

"He's dead, isn't he?" she said flatly.

Tanner didn't reply, so Liz took the initiative.

"Yes."

"How?"

"He was murdered."

"By who?"

This time Tanner answered, making a helpless gesture before he said, "We don't know, Miss Mendez. He was killed before we had a chance to speak with him."

"If he is dead, why did you come?"

"Because he asked for our help."

"And you still wish to help?"

"Yes."

"For what payment?"

"Those arrangements were made with your father."

"But he is dead."

"Nevertheless, those arrangements have been taken care of," Tanner said. "We made a deal and I intend to stick to my part of it."

Liz chose that moment to speak up.

"Miss Mendez, all we want from you right now is an opportunity to care for our horses, clean up, and eat. Then we can talk about how we intend to help."

"Why should I believe that you were hired by my father?"

"Miss Mendez, think about it," Liz said. "Why else would we have come?"

Katarina Mendez looked at them thoughtfully, her eyes lingering longest on Liz. Then she glanced back at Tanner.

"You may call me Katarina," she said.

She looked again at Liz and said, "You may take your horses to the livery, and then go to the hotel. After you have rested there will be food for you in the *cantina.*"

"We're very grateful, Miss — uh, Katarina."

Now she looked at Tanner and said, "If you are lying to me, I will kill you."

Tanner couldn't help but react to that with some amusement.

"All of us?"

"Just you, señor. I will be satisfied with that."

Tanner looked at her, and then nodded his understanding.

She turned and walked away from them, her long legs carrying her in a swift, purposeful stride. Her back was erect and her head held high.

"Wouldn't want to get that hellcat mad at me," Northrop said.

"Then let's not," Tanner told him. "Come on, let's get the horses taken care of."

Liz looked up to the rooftops. The men still had not moved.

They let Liz and Maria off at the hotel, and then went to the livery to care for the horses. To their surprise, there was a woman there who took charge of their horses. She was young and pretty, and Reggie Northrop offered to stay and help her.

"I can care for them myself, señor."

"Come on, Reggie," Tanner said. "Let's stick to the plan."

While the men were at the livery Liz and Maria obtained rooms for everyone. As Liz approached the front desk the woman there hurriedly pushed something down below it. It looked to Liz like she was stuffing a shirt with rags.

It struck her as odd.

The five men returned to the hotel and received their room keys from the woman behind the desk, a handsome woman in her forties.

When Tate entered his room he was surprised to find Liz taking a bath.

"A bathtub in the room?" he exclaimed. "How did you manage that?"

"I'm told that all the rooms have tubs."

"And the water?"

"It was brought by a young girl. I think her mother runs the hotel."

"Interesting," he said.

"Do you want to take a bath?" Liz asked. She stood up so that the water ran off her nipples in little rivulets. Her skin looked shiny and clean, and seeing her like that made Tate lose interest in a bath, but he said, "Yeah. I might as well."

She grinned at him, grabbed a towel, and stepped out of the tub.

Bathed and wearing fresh clothes Tate and Liz came downstairs and met Tanner and Maria.

"Where are the others?" Tate asked.

"They went to the *cantina*," Tanner said. "We're late because we brought women along."

"Ha ha," Liz said. "I had to wait for *Tate* to take a bath."

"And I waited for Chris," Maria said triumphantly.

"Women," Tanner said. "Come on, I'm hungry."

Liz and Maria walked behind the men.

"Have you noticed anything peculiar?" Liz asked after a few minutes, trotting up to join Tate and Tanner.

"Like what?"

"The livery is run by a woman. The hotel is run by a woman. We were met by a woman with a rifle . . ."

"No men," Tanner said.

"Right."

"Maybe they're away?" Tate said.

"Maybe," Liz said.

"What about the men on the rooftops?" Maria asked.

"That's a good question," Liz said. "We can ask Katarina about it."

"The answer should be interesting," Tate said.

CHAPTER NINETEEN

When they reached the *cantina* they found Sanchez, Northrop and Brand already being well feted
by a couple of young women wearing skirts and
peasant blouses. Neither appeared to be more than
eighteen years old.

"That cinches it," Tate said.

"What?" Tanner asked.

Tate inclined his head toward the bar, where
another young woman served as bartender.

"They should call this town *Amazon* Island,"
Tate said under his breath.

A door opened and Katarina Mendez stepped
out.

"Please, sit. The food is ready."

"Thank you," Tate said.

Since Sanchez, Northrop and Brand were sitting
at the same table, Tate, Liz, Tanner and Maria

took another. Quickly, the two women appeared and set steaming plates of meat, vegetables and biscuits before them.

"It looks marvelous," Liz said, and both women smiled at her.

Katarina Mendez kept her distance from them while they ate, but she watched them carefully.

"I think I should be the one to talk to Katarina," Liz said.

"Why?" Tanner asked.

"I think Liz is right," Tate said. "Katarina responded better to Liz on the street."

"What makes you say that?" Tanner demanded, obviously annoyed.

Liz smiled and said, "She didn't threaten to kill me, did she?"

Maria laughed and Tanner said, "Okay, you got me, there. All right, Liz, as long as it works, you can do the talking."

"I also think I know what the story is about the men," she said.

"What's that?" Tanner asked.

"I don't think there are any."

"Well, there certainly aren't any down here, but what about the rooftops?"

"I don't think there are any up there, either."

"We saw them," Maria said.

"We saw hats," Liz said, and then explained what she had seen at the hotel.

"Dummies?" Tanner whispered.

"Old clothes filled with rags, propped up on the rooftops with hats on them. From far off — hell, even from the street — it looks like there are a lot of men up there.''

"It sure does,'' Tanner said.

"You may have something here, Liz,'' Tate said. "After we finish eating we'll — you'll — have a talk with Katarina and we can get the whole story.''

It was only after their plates were cleared and they had been served coffee that Katarina Mendez approached them.

"Can we talk?'' she asked.

"Please join us,'' Liz said, and Tanner pulled a chair over from another table.

"What did my father tell you?''

Briefly Tanner relayed to Katarina the story her father had given him, leaving out the part about the bandits' treasure. From there on, Liz took over.

"Was any of that untrue?'' Liz asked.

"No,'' she said. "My father spoke the truth.''

"Has there been any activity from the *bandidos* since your father has been gone?'' Liz asked.

"They stay on the ridge and watch.''

"The ridge north of town?''

"Yes.''

"None of your people have been bothered by the bandits?'' Tate asked.

"We have not left town, any of us, since my father went to get help.''

"Katarina,'' Liz said, "we're here to help you, why don't you seem pleased?''

"I am sorry,'' Katarina said, "but I only see

seven of you, six with guns. How can you go against so many with so few guns?''

"We have enough to do the job, Katarina, believe me," Liz told her. "Besides, you have people in town who can handle a gun, don't you?''

"We have some, yes."

"The men on the rooftops?" Tate asked, exchanging glances with Liz.

"The men on the rooftops," Katarina said. "We should talk about that."

"There are no men, are there?" Liz asked.

Katarina looked at her somberly and shook her head.

"You mean to say this town is inhabited only by women?" Tanner said.

"Yes."

"No men at all?"

Katarina shook her head.

"Then the men on the roof really are all dummies," Tanner stated matter-of-factly.

"Yes," Katarina said. "My father's idea, to hide the fact that we have no men."

"Where have the men gone?" Liz asked.

"Nowhere," Katarina responded. "We came here to get away from men."

"But your father —"

"My father brought us here," Katarina said. "Myself, and my sisters." She inclined her head to indicate that the two girls who had been serving them were her sisters.

"And the other women?" Liz asked.

"They came later, little by little, until finally we have a population of thirty-four."

"All women," Liz said.

"Except my father . . . and now he is gone."

"But why?"

"You should know," Katarina said to Liz, then looked at Maria and said, "Both of you. Women — especially beautiful women — are targets for men. Many men think they can have anything they want. Those of us who live here are tired of being playthings."

"So you started your own town."

"Yes."

"But now you need our help to solve your problem," Tanner said, and Liz gave him a sharp look.

Katarina, however, responded well.

"And the danger comes from men."

Tanner was about to say something else but Liz stepped on his foot beneath the table. Tanner wasn't sure who had done it, but he kept quiet.

During the awkward silence that followed Katarina glanced at the table where the other three men were sitting, and saw her sisters laughing and talking to Northrop and Sanchez.

"You see?" she said. "It has started already."

"What has?" Tanner asked.

Speaking to Liz, she said, "If you are to stay here and help us, I want you to keep the men away from my sisters — away from all the women. Is that understood?"

"Wait a minute —" Tanner began, but Liz cut him off.

"It's understood, Katarina."

"Good," Katarina said, standing up.

"Katarina, can we talk to you and any others

who can handle a gun a little later?'' Liz asked.

"If you come back in a little while I will have them here. We can talk then.'' She was still speaking directly to Liz, ignoring the men at the table.

She walked over to the other table and herded her sisters away from Northrop and Sanchez.

"What the hell —'' Tanner said. "That is one cold bitch. We're good enough to save their butts, but not good enough to associate with?''

"That's about the size of it, Tanner,'' Liz said. "If you're interested in making a profit on this job, you'll abide by the rules.''

"Oh, he'll abide by the rules,'' Maria said, putting her arm through his.

"And so will Tate,'' Liz said, "but they're not the ones we have to worry about.''

She looked over to the other table. Northrop and Sanchez were watching Katarina and her sisters walk away, and Oren Brand was watching Northrop and Sanchez with some amusement.

CHAPTER TWENTY

Tate, Liz, Tanner and Maria stood up and walked to the table where their partners were sitting.

"Can you believe this town?" Northrop asked. "I've never seen so many pretty women in one place."

"Yeah, well, stay away from them," Tanner said.

"What?" Northrop said. The order also got Sanchez's attention.

"That's a condition of our employment," Liz told them. "You guys stay away from the women."

"You mean we can die for them, but we can't talk to them?" Sanchez asked.

"You've got it now," Liz said.

"Is there enough reward in this to warrant our standing for that?" Northrop demanded.

Now Liz looked at Tanner, who said, "There is."

"That I've got to see!" Northrop exclaimed, eyeing the lady bartender — who seemed to be eyeing him back. In fact, even Katarina's sisters seemed pretty happy to be talking to some men.

"We may have another problem," Liz said to Tanner.

"What?"

She shook her head, indicating that she didn't want to mention it in front of the others.

"You fellas gonna stick around here?" Tanner asked.

"If we're allowed to ask for a deck of cards," Brand muttered.

"We'll be back a little later. We're going to talk to Katarina and whatever other women there are in town who can handle a gun."

"Women handling guns?" Brand said. "You'll excuse me, Liz, but what about the men?"

"There are no men," Liz said.

"No men?" Brand asked incredulously.

"This is a town inhabited entirely by women." She explained about the dummies on the rooftops.

"No wonder," Sanchez said.

"No wonder what?" Tanner asked.

"No wonder those young women —"

"Katarina's sisters," Liz said pointedly.

"Ah," Sanchez said, understanding. "Well, no wonder they couldn't stop talking. They haven't seen a man for . . . how long?"

"A long time," Liz said. "I think we should talk about this," she said to Tanner.

"We'll be back," he said, and Brand got up to go to the bar and ask for a deck of cards.

Outside Tanner said, "What other problem are you worried about, Liz?"

"I'm not so sure that the other women in town feel the way Katarina does."

"What do you mean?"

"That lady bartender wasn't shy about looking Northrop and Sanchez over, and Katarina's sisters certainly didn't seem to mind having men around. If there are other women in town who feel the same way, we may have a problem."

"I still don't —"

"What Liz means," Tate said, "is that we may not have to keep our men away from the women so much as we'll have to keep the women away from our men."

"Oh," Tanner said. "I see what you mean. Tate, maybe we'd better discuss some strategy."

"No women allowed?" Liz asked.

Tanner looked at her and said, "Oh, Liz . . . I didn't mean . . . I thought you and Maria . . ."

"Stop stammering, Tanner," Liz said. "Maria and I will look around town, and then we'll meet you at the hotel before going back to the *cantina*."

"All right," Tanner said, "that sounds fine."

As the two men started for the hotel Maria said, "What are we looking for?"

"Anything," Liz said. "We'll just look around until we find . . . something."

When the women returned from their turn around

town, they found Tate and Tanner in Tanner's room.

"Finished with your strategy session?" Liz asked, pleased that Tanner had the good grace to look embarrassed.

"What did you see around town?"

"Stores, shops, all being run by women," Liz said. "This is not a large town, but neither is it a small town. If they'd allow men in here, they could have a nice little community."

"We also saw the gardens," Maria said. "They grow almost every vegetable imaginable."

"And they slaughter their own meat. We saw the slaughterhouse."

"They even have coffee plants," Maria said.

"They don't have anything coming in from out of town?" Tanner asked.

"If you ask me," Liz said, "what they can't produce themselves, they do without."

"Sounds like they had a nice setup, until the *bandidos* found them," Tate said.

"And now they need us to pull their bacon out of the fire," Tanner said. "That should tell them something."

"Like what?" Liz demanded.

"They need some law here, and a few law*men*. I mean, even if they don't want men to settle here, they could hire some to work for them."

"Well, you can tell Katarina that," Liz said, "if and when we're ready to leave here. And speaking of that, what kind of strategy have you big brains come up with?"

"Our strategy is going to depend a lot on how many guns we can count on from these women," Tate said.

"I guess we'd better get over to the *cantina* and find that out," Tanner said.

"You have never asked me if I can use a gun," Maria said to Tanner accusingly.

Tanner looked at her and realized she was right. Then again, he'd never had any reason to.

"Can you?"

"No," she admitted, "but I can learn."

"You may have to," Liz said.

CHAPTER TWENTY-ONE

Montalvo was in his tent with one of the five women who stayed in camp to keep the men happy. He was running his hands over her breasts, pretending she was Katarina Mendez, when Jaime entered.

"What do you want?" Montalvo demanded.

"I thought you'd want to know . . ."

The woman, Carla, did not bother to hide her nakedness from Jaime. She had been with him many times. In fact, of all the girls, she was his favorite, and she believed he was jealous that she was in Montalvo's tent. She preened for him, holding her breath so that her breasts jutted out.

"Know what?" Montalvo asked.

"Seven riders entered the town a few hours ago."

"A few hours?" Montalvo said, standing. His

erection was huge, and Jaime felt that it was obscene for him to be standing there like that. He also felt a twinge of envy, since he was a much smaller man than Montalvo — in many ways. "Why didn't you tell me this before?"

"I wanted to see if they were staying."

"And?"

"They are."

"Was Mendez with them?"

"No."

"Still, they could be gunmen hired by Mendez to help him."

"Uh, five of them were men, but two were women."

"Two women?"

"Yes, one wearing a gun."

"A woman wearing a gun? Ridiculous."

Montalvo grabbed for his clothes and told Carla, "Get out."

She stood up, pulled a robe around her, and slid past Jaime to leave. Jaime closed his eyes and inhaled her fragrance as she went by.

Montalvo pulled his pants on and said, "What are they doing?"

"It's hard to tell. They moved around from the livery to the hotel to the *cantina*, and then back to the hotel."

"What are they doing now?"

"They are all in the *cantina*, with about twenty of the women from town."

"And the men?"

"They are on the roof."

Montalvo cursed.

"Why is it the only time we see the men is when they are on the rooftops, never in the streets? More and more I feel there is something wrong here, Jaime."

"I agree, Hector," Jaime said. "I think we should go down —"

"Let me think about this for a while," Montalvo said, cutting Jaime off. "Send me some food."

"Sí, I will," Jaime said, wishing that Montalvo would listen to him for once.

"And send me Santos."

Santos again. Jaime was Montalvo's second in command, but more and more he found Hector speaking to Santos in private.

This time he was going to find out why.

CHAPTER TWENTY-TWO

When Liz, Tate, Tanner and Maria reached the *cantina* they found that chairs had been set up as if a show were being put on. About eight women were already seated. They ranged in ages from eighteen to late thirties, and were all attractive.

Northrop, Sanchez and Brand had moved their table out of the way, and were playing poker in a corner.

"Now I know why I prefer American women to Mexican women," Tate said into Liz's ear.

"Why is that?"

"More variety."

Liz saw what he meant. Although the women ranged from the petite to the full bodied, they all had dark skin and black hair. With American women you could count on different skin and hair tones.

"Glad to hear it," she said.

As they entered Katarina approached Liz, who stepped away from Tate.

"Most of the women who can handle a gun are here," she said. "A few more are still coming."

"How many altogether?" Liz asked.

"About twelve."

"Any willing to learn?"

"We are."

The voice belonged to one of Katarina's sisters, although she was obviously speaking for both.

"No," Katarina said.

"Why not?"

"They are —"

"They are in this like everyone else," Liz said.

"We can stay?" the other sister said.

"Yes," Liz said, "you can stay." Katarina pressed her lips firmly together, but said nothing.

Tanner stepped forward, holding a rifle in his left hand.

"When all of the women arrive," Tanner said, "I'll be showing them how to —"

"No."

"What do you mean, no?" he asked Katarina.

"I want Elizabeth to do it."

Tanner looked at Liz and said, "Elizabeth?"

"It is much too pretty a name to be shortened," Katarina said.

"Thank you . . . Katarina," Liz said.

Tate walked to the back where the poker game was going on.

"Room for another hand?" he asked.

"Aren't you and Tanner gonna give lessons in handling a gun?" Brand asked.

"That'll be taken care of by Liz and Tanner," Tate said, pulling up a chair.

"Why's that?"

"Our employer — that is, our employer's daughter — seems to trust Liz more than any one of us men."

"I'd like to get that Katarina into a hotel room bed. I could change her mind in a hurry," Northrop said.

"And her sweet young sisters . . ." Sanchez said, fairly salivating.

"Down, boy," Tate said, "and deal the cards."

"They're all here," Katarina said to Liz.

Liz surveyed her audience and found it made up of eighteen women. Twelve of them had some working knowledge of guns. The other six wanted to learn — as did Maria, who had joined them.

Tanner spoke briefly, introducing himself, explaining who he and the others were and why they were there. Then he turned them over to Liz. For want of something better to do, he joined the poker game.

Liz spoke briefly but expertly about handguns and rifles. As he listened, Tate couldn't help but be proud of her, since most of what she knew she had learned from him.

"Now, tomorrow morning we'll set up some targets for you to practice on," Liz said. "Those of you who don't have guns, we'll find some for you. That's all."

As the women stood up, preparing to leave, Katarina came up to Liz.

"I want to thank you for your help," she said.

"It's more than just me," Liz said.

"Look at them," the Mexican woman said, her distaste evident in her voice. "All men want to do is gamble, drink, and debauch women."

"I don't think —"

"You are an intelligent woman, Elizabeth," Katarina said. "Surely they do not have you fooled."

"No one has me fooled, Katarina. But I can't condemn all men."

"You will see," Katarina said, "you will see."

As Katarina walked to the door in the back wall Liz went over to the poker game.

"I feel sorry for her," she said.

"For who?" Tate asked.

"Katarina. She really hates men — all men. It's making her very bitter."

"I could fix that," Northrop said.

"No better than I could," Sanchez boasted.

Liz looked at both of them, then said, "Although in some cases, she's probably right." She turned on her heels and stalked out of the *cantina*.

"What's the matter with her?" Northrop asked.

"Deal me out," Tate said, and went to find out.

CHAPTER TWENTY-THREE

Jaime was hiding behind Montalvo's tent when Santos entered.

"You wanted to see me, Hector?" Santos asked.

Jaime had thought he was the only one who called Montalvo by his first name.

"Ah, Santos, good. Here, have a drink."

Jaime was startled to hear something being poured. Montalvo had never offered him a drink.

"What did you want to see me about, Hector?" Santos asked.

"Are you still seeing that girl from the town?"

"As you have told me to, yes. She does not know much, though. She is not related to Katarina, you know. It would be better if I could become friendly with one of Katarina's sisters —"

"Better, yes, but not likely."

"Do you wish me to stop seeing her?"

"No, I want you to try and get some information

out of her about the people who arrived today. I want to know who they are."

"And why they are here?"

Montalvo snorted.

"I think we know why they are here, Santos."

"Because of us?" Santos asked. "What can five men hope to do —"

"If they are the same men — and I am sure they are — then they have already killed some of our men."

"They were taken by surprise —"

"The men were careless, they deserved to die. I am not careless. I want to know who I am dealing with before I make a move. That is where your girlfriend comes in. *Comprende?*"

"Sí, Hector. I will find out what I can."

"Good, very good. Santos, you are coming closer and closer to the day when you will be my right hand."

"I look forward to that day, *Jefe.*"

"Go now."

Santos left, and Jaime sat down on the ground behind Montalvo's tent. He had been loyal to Hector Montalvo for many years, and this was how he was to be paid back.

Well, now that he knew this treachery was afoot, he had to figure out what to do about it.

After Santos left Montalvo poured himself another drink. Santos was the best looking man in his ranks, but he had no brains. He could make as many promises as he wanted to the man, and Santos would continue to believe him.

A man like that was very useful to have around.

CHAPTER TWENTY-FOUR

"What's wrong?" Tate asked when he caught up to Liz on her way to the hotel.

Liz looked at him and said, "The problem is that all men are not like you."

"That's a problem?" he asked. "Some people would call that a blessing."

"Oh, I don't mean that you're perfect . . ."

"Thanks," he said wryly.

"But you're not like those two or like the men that Katarina has obviously met."

"What kind of men are those?"

"The kind that can take a lovely, vibrant woman like her and turn her into a bitter spinster."

"She doesn't look like a spinster to me."

"She will in a few years. I don't like that idea."

"And you think it was men like Northrop and Sanchez who made her like that?"

"Men like them, but worse. There is something

. . . charming about them, in a childish way, but with just a little push they could become boorish, oily looking men . . ." She trailed off because words failed her.

"Have you met men like that?"

"Some," she said, "but obviously not as many as Katarina has."

"What else is bothering you?"

"This town," she said, annoyed. "It's not right. It's not right for a group of attractive women to hide themselves away like this."

"Well, maybe some of the women agree with you."

"If we could get them out from under this danger, maybe they could make their own decisions about that."

"You think Katarina will let them? I mean, she pretty much looks like the leader here. I think she was, even when her father was alive."

"She'll want what's best for them."

"What about what's best for her?"

"What do you mean?"

"By keeping them here she stays in power. If they leave, she'll have no one to lead."

"You think she's like that?"

"I think she could be."

"You think she needs a good man?"

"Maybe," he said. "Unfortunately, there are none available."

They were at the entrance to the hotel and she turned and grabbed him by the front of his shirt with both hands.

"You've got that right."

CHAPTER TWENTY-FIVE

Reggie Northrop frowned as he undressed for bed. A town full of women — attractive women — and he was forbidden even to talk to them.

Bullshit.

Tomorrow he was going to pick one out and go after her. He would have liked to see how he could do with Maria, but she was Tanner's woman. No matter. There were plenty of others around.

Northrop's room overlooked a back alley, and he had barely gotten between the sheets when he heard someone at his window trying to get it open. He leapt out of bed, yanked his gun from his holster, and walked over to the window. Flattening himself against the wall, he waited.

Finally, whoever was working on the window got it open and started to enter the room. When an arm appeared Northrop grabbed it and dragged the intruder into the room. Pointing his gun menacingly, Northrop said, "Who are you?"

The intruder looked up at him and Northrop found himself staring into the beautiful face of one of the young girls who had been serving the food at the *cantina*.

Pete Sanchez always slept very badly, so he was immediately aware of the fact that someone was opening his door. It was easy, because his room did not have a lock. Slowly, he took his gun from beneath his pillow and when he had a firm grip on it he sat up in bed and snapped out, "Don't move!"

"Don't shoot," a voice said — a woman's voice.

He waited while the shadowy figure reached up to the lamp next to the door and turned the light up ever so slightly.

Sanchez found himself looking at the beautiful bartender from the *cantina*.

Oren Brand's door *did* have a lock on it, but that didn't stop whoever was at his door. Someone obviously had a key, Brand realized, and was fitting it into the lock as quietly as possible — but not quietly enough.

Brand was across the room before the door opened, and he pulled his unexpected visitor into the room with such force that they both ended up on the bed.

Brand reached for the lamp and turned it up.

"What the —" he said.

On his bed was one of the girls from the *cantina*.

"What are you doing here?"

She smiled and removed her hat, letting her long, silky black hair fall down to her shoulders.

"I have been a long time without a man," she said to him.

Brand frowned, then walked over to her and reached for her. She misunderstood his intention, and was surprised when he pulled her off the bed and propelled her toward the door.

"What —" she said.

He sat down on the bed and put his gun back in his holster. He was wearing only his long underwear, and felt acutely uncomfortable with her in the room.

"Out," he said. "I've got to get some sleep."

She was wearing pants and a large, oversized shirt with the tails hanging out.

"Why do you want me to leave?" she asked. "I want to make love with you."

Brand couldn't believe his ears. This girl couldn't have been more than eighteen. He was thirty goddamn years older than she was!

"Girl, I'm old enough to be your grandfather!" he exclaimed. "Go and knock on Northrop's door, or Sanchez's."

"I do not want them," she protested. "I want you."

"I'm an old man."

She unbuttoned her shirt and let it hang open. He could see her small breasts and her smooth dark skin. Brand felt the burgeoning between his legs, and she saw it.

"Not so old," she said.

"Did you hear something?" Liz asked Tate.

She had broken a kiss to ask him that, and Tate pulled her back down to him.

"I didn't hear a thing," he said.

"My name is Vita," the girl said.

Brand watched as she allowed her shirt to fall off her shoulders to the floor. Her breasts were small and firm, like peaches, and her nipples were dark brown. Next she removed the soft shoes she was wearing, then unbuttoned her jeans and slid them down her hips, revealing that she was wearing no underwear. The tangle of dark hair between her legs glistened slightly, and he could already smell her readiness.

She walked across the room to him and slid into his lap, rubbing her smooth butt against the large erection under his long underwear.

"W-why me?" Brand managed to stammer.

"Because you are a real man," she said. "You are not pretty like the others. My sister wanted Northrop, and my cousin wanted the other pretty one, Sanchez. I wanted you."

"But —" he started. Before he could utter another sound, she pulled his face to her breasts.

Her skin was incredibly soft, and her fragrance intoxicated him. He touched his tongue to one nipple, and it sprang to life immediately. Gently he bit it. As Vita moaned and cradled his head he became bolder, rolling her nipple with his tongue, sucking it, and then switching to the other breast.

Finally, Vita pulled his head up and kissed him. She smelled and tasted so sweet that Brand responded immediately. He put his strong arms around her, pulling her tightly against him. If not for her breasts pressing into his chest, she might have been a small child curled up in his lap. He could feel the heat of her body right through his underwear.

Vita moaned and opened her mouth wide, drawing Brand's tongue inside. She shifted around on his lap so that she could reach between them, unbutton his underwear, and pull out his throbbing cock.

From there she slid to her knees. Brand couldn't believe it when she took him in her mouth. It felt as if he were sliding his cock into a vat of hot butter.

Vita's sister, Lily, reached for Northrop's butt and gripped him tightly with both hands as he drove into her. She kissed his neck, then slid her lips along his shoulder until, as she was about to come, she sank her teeth into him to keep from screaming.

Vita and Lily's cousin, Pilar, was twenty-four, and although she might not have been Sanchez's first choice, he certainly did not kick her out of bed.

She was so eager that as soon as his lips and teeth touched her nipples she came, shuddering in his arms. Sanchez mounted her then and slid into her fully. She wrapped her legs around his hips and they began to move together, slowly at first, and then faster.

"I know I heard something," Liz said, sitting up in bed.

"Yeah," Tate said, "I did, too."

"It sounds like . . ."

They both listened intently, and then Liz said, "Tanner and Maria?"

"They're on the other end of the floor."

"Who's next door?"

"Sanchez."

Liz got up from the bed and walked to the wall, pressing her ear against it. She distinctly heard a man and a woman in the throes of passion.

"Is it . . ." Tate said.

Liz turned and looked at him.

"We can't let Katarina know about this."

"We don't even know who's in there with him."

"It doesn't matter," Liz said, returning to the bed. "These women have gone a long time without men. For all we know the same thing can be happening in the other rooms, as well."

"You want to go and listen in at the doors?"

"You're not taking this seriously enough."

"Liz, what is she going to do, fire us? Then who's going to save her town for her?"

"Let's just keep it quiet. Maybe we can talk to the men in the morning."

"Sure," Tate said, "I'll talk to them, but I don't think it's going to do much good."

Although she said nothing, Liz didn't think so, either.

Vita sat astride Oren Brand, his erection buried deep inside her. She leaned over so he could suck on her breasts and bite her nipples as she writhed on him. Every so often she'd make a low, squeaking sound, as if she were trying to keep from crying out.

When she sat up straight and began grinding herself down on him, Brand could see her face. He had never before been with a woman as beautiful as this one, and at that moment he didn't care how old she was or where they were.

He only cared that they were together.

Brand watched Vita as she dressed. She had not seemed very experienced, but she had known all the right things to do. It was as if she had been told by someone, but was actually doing them for the first time.

God, he thought, could it possibly get even better?

She kissed him softly before leaving and said, "For a powerful man, you are very tender. I will come again."

"Vita, it might not be right —"

She put her forefinger to his lips and said, "I will come again."

Later the two sisters and their cousin sneaked out of the hotel together, giggling and exchanging stories about the men they had been with. They all knew what would happen if Katarina found out, but they didn't care. They hated this town, and had been too long without men.

Pilar, being the oldest, was the most experienced one, and she had told the sisters, Vita and Lily, exactly what to do.

She was very proud of them when they told her how things had gone.

All three women hoped that the men would stay alive for at least a few days.

Maybe even as long as a week.

From a doorway Katarina Mendez watched as her sisters and cousin went back to their rooms above the *cantina*. When she was sure they wouldn't see her she stepped out of the shadows and began walking to her house.

CHAPTER TWENTY-SIX

In the morning Tate and Liz rose and went downstairs.

"Sure," Liz said when they discovered they were alone, "the others must be exhausted."

"Now Liz, we only know of one for sure who had a woman in his room."

"We can find out about the others soon enough."

"What time are you going to drill the women with their guns?" Tate asked.

"I don't know. About ten, why?"

"I've got an idea, but we'll have to talk to Katarina about it."

"Why don't we have breakfast first, and you can explain it to me?"

"All right."

As it turned out, there was no place for them to

get breakfast that early in the morning. They finally went back to the hotel to ask the woman behind the desk about it.

"At nine, señor, you can get breakfast at the *cantina*," she said, speaking to Tate, eyeing him up and down with obvious appreciation.

"Thank you," he said, and they went outside again.

"That one would have liked to visit your room last night," Liz said to him. "I wonder if she knows about the others?"

"Probably. How could they have gotten past her?"

Liz could think of a few ways, but there was no point in speculating.

"Let's take a turn around town and you can explain your idea to me," she suggested.

Walking around town, they eventually stopped at the northern end. They gazed up at the ridge where they figured the bandits' lookout must be.

"What do you think they make of us?" Liz asked.

"Five men and two women ride into town and stay? They're probably confused by you and Maria, but they've got to figure that the five men are here to work."

"By now they know about the men we killed."

"Too much of a coincidence not to have been us," Tate said. "No, I think they know why we're here. Now what they're wondering is who we are."

"Let them wonder," Liz said. "I'm hungry."

By the time they finished their walk, the *cantina* was open. They entered and found the same woman behind the bar that they had met there the day before.

"Can we get some breakfast?" Liz asked.

"Of course, señorita. I will have Vita and Lily prepare it."

"Are they Katarina's sisters?"

"Si, señorita, and I am their cousin. My name is Pilar."

"When will Katarina awake?" Liz asked.

"Soon."

"Does she live back there?" Liz asked, indicating the door at the back of the room.

"No, she has a house on the edge of town."

"Which edge?" Tate asked.

"The north. It is a yellow house."

"All right, thank you," Liz said.

"I will bring coffee right out," Pilar said.

True to her word she brought out two cups and a pot and promised that breakfast would follow.

"Are eggs all right?" she asked.

"Fine."

"Well?" Tate said when Pilar left them alone.

"I like your idea. It makes sense."

"You better propose it to Katarina. I don't think she'll like it coming from me."

"You're probably right," Liz admitted. "In fact, I think I'll go to her house and talk to her."

As she stood up Tate said, "What about breakfast?"

"Keep it warm for me," Liz said. She started to

walk away, then came back and said, "The same doesn't go for the girls."

"Get out of here."

CHAPTER TWENTY-SEVEN

Liz couldn't miss the yellow house. She knocked and when Katarina answered the door, it was obvious that she had been up for some time. Her face looked well scrubbed, and she was dressed.

"Oh, good morning, Elizabeth."

"Good morning, Katarina. May I speak to you?"

"Of course."

When they were in the house Liz saw a pot of water on the stove.

"I was going to have some tea, but if you prefer coffee —"

"No, tea is fine, thank you."

"Please, sit."

Liz sat at the handmade wooden table while Katarina busied herself with the tea. Soon, she came to the table with two cups, and sat down opposite Liz.

"I know that my sisters and my cousin visited your hotel last night."

"They did?"

"You didn't know?"

"I knew that someone had come to the hotel to see one of the men," Liz said honestly, "but I didn't know who, or how many."

"Three," she said. "My cousin, Pilar, is more experienced. I'm sure it was her idea."

"Not all of the women here feel the same as you do about men?"

"Obviously not. I have tried to teach my sisters, but —"

"They'll have to form their own opinions, Katarina," Liz said.

"I know, that is why I am not making a fuss about their visits."

"You think that by sleeping with these men, they'll come to agree with you?"

"They will form their own opinions, and then we can talk about them."

Liz couldn't think of anything to say that wouldn't have been . . . well, insulting.

"You did not think I could be that reasonable?" Katarina asked.

"Frankly, no."

"I am not so rigid in my thinking, Elizabeth."

"About men?"

"That is a different matter. I have never met a man who did not disappoint me. I have come to prefer the company of women."

Liz wondered exactly what Katarina meant by that.

"But you did not come here to discuss my family problems. Have you come up with a plan?"

"An idea, for now."

"Which is?"

"When I drill the women today, Katarina, I would like them to dress like men. Wear their hair up inside their hats, that kind of thing."

Katarina hesitated a moment, then said, "That makes sense. From the ridge it will simply look as if our men are practicing."

"That's correct."

"An excellent idea, Elizabeth."

Liz almost told her that it was Tate's, then decided not to. She wanted to keep her relationship with Katarina exactly the way it was.

Liz finished her tea and stood up.

"I will come to the *cantina* shortly," Katarina said. "The women will gather there. Where would you like to drill?"

Liz thought a moment, then said, "Why fool around? Let's do it on the main street."

"Another excellent idea," Katarina said. "I believe my father was right to hire you."

Again, Liz kept the truth to herself, that she had never met Katarina's father, and that even Tanner — who had been the one Mendez had hired — did not know about her until he met with Tate.

"I'll see you in a little while," Liz said.

Katarina opened the door for her and then put her hand on Liz's shoulder. Her touch felt almost like a caress.

"Thank you for your help."

Liz wanted to say, "It's being paid for," but thought that might sound too harsh. Instead she simply nodded and slid from beneath Katarina's touch.

When Liz returned to the *cantina* she found Tate having a cup of coffee. There was no sign of breakfast on the table, and seated across from him was the bartender, Pilar. When she saw Liz enter, the Mexican girl hurriedly rose and returned to the bar.

"How was breakfast?" Liz asked.

"Fine. Pilar says she'll have the girls bring you a hot breakfast if you want."

"I'll bet."

"What took you so long?"

"Katarina invited me in for a cup of tea."

"How did she like the idea?"

"She complimented me on it. She thought it was an excellent idea."

"She wouldn't if she knew it was mine."

"You didn't seem to mind staying behind and losing the credit."

"What are you — oh, you mean Pilar?"

"Pilar who?" Liz asked, picking up his coffee cup and draining it.

CHAPTER TWENTY-EIGHT

Montalvo came up behind Jaime and asked, "What is going on down there?"

"Looks like they're practicing."

"Practicing what?"

"Practicing with guns."

"They have never done that before," Montalvo said, peering down at the town in confusion.

"Well, you wanted to know who the new people were," Jaime said. "One of them is drilling them with their guns."

"Which one?"

"The blonde woman."

"The woman?" Montalvo asked in disbelief.

"They look like they are getting ready to fight us."

Montalvo laughed behind him, a loud, harsh sound.

"And they are learning from a woman?" Montalvo said. "They intend to put up quite a fight, I see."

"I would not laugh, Hector," Jaime warned.

"Why not?"

Jaime looked at his leader and said, "The woman looks like she knows what she is doing."

"Bah!" Montalvo said. "What danger could a woman be to us?"

"I do not think this is an ordinary woman, Hector," Jaime said.

"What do you mean?"

"I have heard stories about a yellow-haired woman who is very deadly with a gun. They say she has the eyes of an angel, and can send a man to the devil without even blinking."

"Such a woman cannot exist," Montalvo said. "When we take the town I will strip that woman naked in front of everyone and show her what a woman is for. Keep watching, Jaime."

"I will keep watching," Jaime said.

They managed to scrounge up enough rifles and handguns for all of the women to practice. The women were wearing jeans and oversized shirts, and had hats on with their hair tucked underneath. Up close they looked like women trying to dress like men, but from a distance Liz figured they'd pass well enough.

She and Tate approached Tanner with the idea that Liz would drill them alone.

"It will confuse the enemy," Liz said.

"It's a good idea," Tanner said.

While she worked with the women, Tate and Tanner visited the shops in town to see if there was anything they could put to good use in setting up a defense.

To Liz's surprise, Katarina insisted on taking part in the drills, but it came as no surprise that she was one of the quickest students.

"Take a break," Liz told the women after they'd worked for several hours. "Come back in an hour."

As the women scattered, Katarina came over to Liz and said, "How are they doing?"

"We can put them up on the rooftops," Liz said. "As long as they can shoot, they're liable to hit something."

"I know some of them can't shoot very well —"

"We'll find shotguns for those who can't," Liz said. "It's hard to miss with a shotgun."

"What are we going to do?" Katarina asked. "Sit here and wait until they attack us?"

"They haven't attacked in all this time," Liz said, "but that could mean one of two things."

"What?"

"One, they don't want to attack, and will hold off as long as they can."

"That gains them nothing."

"Especially since you're not letting your people out of town," Liz said. "That brings us to two."

"Which is?"

"Any day now they'll decide to stop waiting and come on down. We have to be ready for them if they do."

"We will be ready," Katarina said emphatically.

"Yeah," Liz said. "Go take a break, Katarina, and then come back with the others."

CHAPTER TWENTY-NINE

"Break time?" Oren Brand asked as Liz entered the *cantina*.

She nodded.

"How are they doing?" Northrop inquired. Once again he, Brand and Sanchez were playing poker.

Liz made a face.

"We'll just have to put them on the rooftops and take our chances."

"Do you know what Tanner is planning?" Sanchez asked.

"No. All I know is I'm supposed to get those women to the point where they won't shoot off a toe, or shoot each other."

"Where are —" Brand started to ask, but at that point Tate and Tanner entered, each carrying a wooden crate.

"What have we here?" Liz asked.

They each set a crate on an empty table and Tanner said, "Dynamite. Who knows how to handle this stuff?"

"I do," Brand said.

"Okay, fine. You're in charge."

"Let's get it off the tables and in the back somewhere," he said.

He picked up one crate while Tate took the other. Pilar showed them where the storeroom was.

Tanner approached the poker table and said, "We've got something to talk about."

"What?" Sanchez asked, looking as innocent as possible.

"Let's wait for the others."

When Tate and Brand returned Brand sat back down at the table and Tate remained standing.

"Liz tells me she had a talk with Katarina this morning," Tanner said.

"What about?" Brand asked.

"You three. Katarina says that some of the women visited you last night."

There was no reply.

"Is that true?"

"Yes," Sanchez admitted.

"Yes," Northrop said, exchanging surprised looks with Sanchez.

"Yes," Brand said as both Northrop and Sanchez looked at him in utter disbelief.

"Did any of you plan this?"

"No," they all answered.

"She came through my window," Northrop said. "She begged for it."

"The rest of you?"

"Mine came to the door, but otherwise the same applies," Brand said.

"Same here," Sanchez said.

Tanner shook his head.

"We don't need that kind of complication on this job," he said. "You should have sent them away."

"That's easy for you to say," Northrop snapped. "You and Tate brought your women with you."

Before Tanner could reply, Brand said, "I don't know about the others, but I sure haven't had a pretty young woman throw herself into my lap in a long time. I'd've had to be inhuman to turn her away."

Tanner looked at Brand and then said, "All right, I can understand that."

"How did Katarina take it?" Northrop asked.

"Considering that two of the girls are her sisters and the other is her cousin, she took it quite well, but I hope you fellas don't intend to make a habit of it."

"I'd say that's up to the women," Northrop said.

"All right, let's forget that for now," Tanner said. He looked at Tate and Liz and said, "Pull up a couple of chairs."

"Where's Maria?" Liz asked.

"She doesn't need to be here for this."

"I expected her to be at the drill earlier."

"Uh, she couldn't," Tanner said, looking slightly embarrassed. "How did that go, by the way?"

Realizing Tanner probably wouldn't let Maria come to the practice session, Liz gave him the same report she had given Katarina and the other three hired guns. Tanner made a face.

"We'll have to make the best of it."

Liz just nodded.

"I need someone to go up on the ridge and scout the bandits," Tanner said. "I'd go, but I'm like a bull in a china shop. Sanchez, you move like an Indian."

"Sure, I'll go," he said.

"Anyone else?"

"I'll go."

They all looked at the person who had spoken — Liz.

"You?" Tanner said.

"Yeah, I'm pretty stealthy."

"Stealthy?" Northrop repeated.

"She reads a lot of books," Tate said, "learns a big word now and again."

"I don't think —" Tanner began.

"Look, I'm here to take an equal share of the work."

"You're running the drills," Tanner said. "That's work enough."

"That's in the daytime," she said. "I assume you want this little reconnaissance maneuver to take place tonight after dark."

"That's right."

"Well, I've hunted wolves before, I don't suppose this will be much different."

Tanner looked at Tate, but before Tate could say or do anything Liz broke in.

"Don't be looking to Tate for approval. He's got nothing to say about it. It's between you and me."

That drew some laughter and Sanchez said, "She's got you there, Tanner."

Tanner frowned. It went against the grain for him to use a woman for such a job, but Sanchez would be with her, and Sanchez was a good man.

"All right," he said finally. "Liz and Pete."

"What do you want to know?" Liz asked.

"How many, what kind of firepower they've got, how much supplies they've got. It would help us to know how well fixed they are to stay up there for a long time."

Sanchez looked at Liz and said, "How's midnight sound to you?"

She smiled at him and said, "It's a date."

He grinned back and said, "I wish."

CHAPTER THIRTY

Liz and Sanchez met at the *cantina* at a quarter to midnight. Sanchez was sorry he was going to miss Pilar's visit — or was his Lily? — that night, but being with Liz alone was almost worth it. If he could just catch her interest . . .

"The others have all turned in," Sanchez said.

"Who's on watch?"

"Brand. Shall we go?" Sanchez asked.

"Let's."

"I'm sorry I didn't bring you any flowers."

"I forgive you."

They walked in the shadows to the north end of town, passing the livery on the way and finally coming to Katarina's yellow house. It was completely dark.

"The ice lady is asleep."

"That's not called for," Liz said.

"I don't know about you, but I feel a definite chill whenever that lady is in the room."

Liz decided not to argue the point.

"Which way?" she asked.

"I figure they have a man on watch right up on the ridge. This is no mountain, but it is a long way up. Let's move to the right here and see if we can find a passable way up."

Hiding in the shadows cast by Katarina's house they moved to the right and eventually came to the base of the hill that overlooked the town.

It took over an hour, and at one point they had to double back and look for a better way, but eventually they reached the top. They found some thick foliage and took cover in it.

"Let's lie still and see what we can hear." Sanchez suggested.

"All right," Liz agreed.

It sounded like a good idea to her, even though she knew Sanchez was enjoying the close proximity they were forced into.

They lay hip to hip, thigh to thigh, and Sanchez was indeed enjoying the heat he felt from her body. Was she becoming aroused, he wondered . . . as he was?

How would she react if he proposed a little clinch in the bushes?

"What's that?" she asked.

"What?" He hadn't been listening. He'd been busy inhaling her scent.

"Listen," she hissed.

He gave his attention to whatever sounds might

be travelling through the night air, and he too heard it.

"Voices," he whispered.

She nodded and said, "That's what I thought."

"Let's follow the sound. We may just find ourselves a bandit camp."

They were far enough away from the edge of the ridge to avoid the lookout. They stayed within the trees as much as possible, and Sanchez was impressed with Liz's ability to move silently. She was beautiful, intelligent, and she moved like an Indian.

He wondered idly exactly how devoted she really was to Tate.

"Easy," he said at one point. "We're getting close."

They moved forward, and when Sanchez pushed apart two bushes, they were looking directly at the bandit camp.

There were two tents and at least three campfires. At this time of night it was difficult to make an accurate count, but there seemed to be at least thirty or forty men.

"Okay," Sanchez said, "one tent will be for the big leader —"

"And the other for ammunition."

He looked at her and said, "Yes, and supplies. If we can get a look inside that second tent, we'd know how well stocked they are."

"Then let's get it done," she said, starting to move forward.

"What do you intend to do?" he asked, putting his hand on her arm to stay her.

"Use a knife to cut a back door into the tent. Then one of us can stand watch while the other one goes in."

"Wait. If we do that they'll discover that cut in the tent and know that we've been here."

"So what?" she said. "They know we're in town. If they think that we came up here without them hearing us, it'll only hurt their ego."

He stared at her a moment, then said, "You are right. I'm impressed."

"Thanks."

"You see if you can get a better head count and I'll go in."

"No, it was my idea," she said. "You take the count and I'll go in."

He shook his head slowly and said, "You really don't need me up here at all, do you?"

"Sure I do."

"You do?"

She nodded and put her hand out.

"Can I borrow your knife?"

CHAPTER THIRTY-ONE

Liz applied the razor-sharp edge of Sanchez's knife to the fabric of the tent. It split almost soundlessly. She ran the knife all the way down until she had a cut she could easily step through.

Inside the tent she immediately realized she had a problem. It was pitch dark, without even moonlight to illuminate her way. She froze for a moment, waiting for her eyes to adjust, and hoping that she would be able to make out what she needed to see. Soon she could see shapes and sizes, but she still was unable to discern contents. Liz knew she couldn't risk lighting a match. That would give her away immediately.

She began moving slowly about the tent, peering forward intently to avoid tripping on anything. After a few moments, using her hands and what little night vision she had, she was able to ascertain that the guns and ammunition were on one side while the food stores were on the other. The boxes were stacked taller than she was on both sides, and despite the darkness she felt fairly certain that she'd be able to guess at how much ammo and food they had. If Sanchez could get a better head count on the men themselves, they'd be able to tell how long the bandits would be able to stay up here.

Suddenly she heard the sound of two men talking. The voices seemed to be approaching the tent.

Frantically she searched for cover. Moving to her left, she banged her shin on a box and bit back the cry of pain that welled up in her throat. Cursing silently she crouched down behind a stack of boxes and waited.

The front flap of the tent was thrown back and the inside was bathed in a soft, dim light thrown from the campfires outside. A lone man entered, went to the food stores and removed a few cans. He was about to leave when he froze and turned around.

Had he heard her? Had he somehow seen the tear in the rear of the tent?

Apparently not, because the next moment he shrugged and exited the tent.

Liz wasted no time in vacating her hiding place and sliding through the cut in the rear of the tent. As soon as she stepped through she heard something, but was too slow to react. An arm snaked around her neck. Suddenly her air was cut off and she couldn't breathe.

"I thought I saw something, but I was not sure," a man said in Spanish. It must have been the man who had entered the tent. "I had no idea I would find something so . . . pleasant." His other hand came around and closed over one of Liz's breasts. "*Qué linda!*" he said.

She could have reached her gun, but the sound of a shot would have brought the whole camp down on her. As the man slid his hand inside her shirt and squeezed her breast, laughing softly in her ear, she took out Sanchez's knife and stabbed backward, hoping that she would hit a vital spot.

The man grunted in surprise as the knife bit into him, and he released her. Quickly pulling the knife free, Liz turned and slashed at his throat before he could cry out. Blood flowed over the front of his shirt and he opened his mouth as if to scream, but he made no sound. His eyes grew wider and wider until suddenly they went blank and he slumped to the ground. Unable to support his weight, she had to step back as he collapsed and hope that no one heard him fall.

Liz ran straight back into the brush and hunkered down. She was supposed to head for the prearranged meeting place with Sanchez, but she was faced with a dilemma. From what Tanner had said — or what he had been told by Katarina's father — there was supposed to be a cave up here where the bandits kept a treasure. She and Sanchez had been traipsing around for the better part of an hour and she hadn't seen any cave. Of course, the mouth of the cave could have been well hidden. Should she mention the cave to Sanchez? As far as she knew, only she, Tate and Tanner knew about it.

Finally, she decided that they had what they had come for and they shouldn't push their luck.

She went to meet Sanchez.

"Santa Maria," he said as she joined him, "what took you so long? You're covered with blood!"

She looked down and saw that some of the man's blood had splashed onto her. Shivering involuntarily, she realized that her shirt was matted to her chest by his blood. If only she could remove it and take a bath.

"I got caught," she said, "and put your knife to good use." Quickly, she explained what happened.

"I knew it," he said. "I should have stood watch while you went inside."

"Don't blame yourself. We agreed that you'd get a head count. Speaking of which, did you get one?" she asked.

"I think so."

"Then we're finished here," she said. "Let's get out of here before someone finds that man's body."

"The date's over, huh?" he asked, grinning.

She grinned back, and they started back down to town.

CHAPTER THIRTY-TWO

When Brand finished his watch he went back to his room and found Vita waiting for him. She was naked in his bed, and as he walked in she pulled the sheet back to show him.

"Vita, this isn't a secret anymore," he said.

"I don't care," she told him, getting up on her knees. She ran her hands over her small breasts and said. "I want you, Oren."

Looking at her like that, feeling the heat in his groin, he didn't much care, either.

Northrop was thoroughly enjoying his time with Lily this evening. He knew he'd have to get her out of the room, though, before it was time for his watch. He didn't want to be caught by Tate or Tanner. It wasn't that he was afraid of them, but he had to work with them, and avoiding a confrontation would make that easier.

Looking down at her face as he drove into her, he wondered if there were any other women in town who might want to be where she was now.

Tanner couldn't sleep, so he simply stared at the ceiling and listened to Maria's breathing. She had been angry with him when he wouldn't allow her to drill with the other women, but he wanted to keep her out of the line of fire. Luckily, since she was his woman, she considered it her duty to obey him.

You didn't find many women like that anymore, he thought.

He decided to stop worrying about his private life while there was still one more job to be done.

Sending Liz and Sanchez up to spy on the bandits meant that the operation really was in progress. Depending on what they brought back, plans could be made. He had no intentions of waiting around for the bandits to make the first move.

He wanted to get this over with as soon as possible, take his pay and go off somewhere with Maria.

On watch, Tate was worrying about Liz. He knew she could handle herself, but that didn't mean he wasn't going to worry about her. He hoped that the bandits' treasure was a large one. With what he and Liz could make from this job, they could go somewhere, settle down, and never have to worry about one another again.

CHAPTER THIRTY-THREE

Liz and Sanchez made their way down from the bandit camp, staying in the shadows until they were alongside the livery.

"We'd better get some sleep," Sanchez said. "We can give all of this to Tanner in the morning."

"Wait a minute," Liz said.

"What is it?"

"I hear something."

He listened and heard the same thing. The sounds of a man and woman, inside the livery.

"Wonder who that is?"

"So do I," Liz said. "Both Brand and Northrop have a room for that sort of thing. You five are supposed to be the only men in town."

For a moment Sanchez fantasized that it was Tate, not wanting to use the room that he and Liz shared. Finding her man with a young Mexican girl might then drive Liz Archer right into Sanchez's bed.

"Maybe we should check," he said.

"Maybe we should," she agreed. "We'll have to be real quiet. I think I remember a lamp on a hook just inside the livery door."

"If the door's not locked . . ." he said.

It wasn't locked, and as they opened it carefully it didn't make so much as a squeak. Liz groped for the lamp, found it, struck a match and stared at the spectacle in front of her.

There was a man and a girl, both naked, lying on a bed of hay. The man's buttocks were rising and falling with increasing speed, and both were so near orgasm that neither of them realized that they were being watched.

"Oh Jesus, oh Jesus," the man was muttering, grunting as he drove into the girl.

All they could see of her was her brown arms and legs, but they could hear her crying out, *"Díos mio, Díos mio,"* over and over again.

Finally they both climaxed, moaning and groaning, the girl calling out "Santos" again and again.

Sanchez was acutely aware of the fact that he had a huge, painful erection that was trying to burst out of his pants. He wished he had the nerve to throw Liz down on a similar bed of hay, but he didn't think she'd go for that.

"Nice performance," Liz said aloud, "but it's time to get up now."

The man did not even look behind him. He

pushed himself off the girl and groped for his gun, which was in a holster lying near him.

"I wouldn't!" Liz yelled, drawing her own weapon.

The man froze, his hand inches from the gun.

The girl sat up and stared at them, making no move to cover her naked breasts. Sanchez's erection began to throb, and he was afraid to move for fear that he would soil his pants.

"That's the girl who works the livery," Liz said.

"So it is," Sanchez muttered, staring at the girl's breasts.

"Turn around so we can see who you are," Liz said to the man.

Slowly the man turned over. His damp, semi-erect penis had hay sticking to it. He was a good-looking man in his thirties with a long, black mustache and curly black hair on his chest.

"You know what I think we have here, Pete?" Liz said.

"No, what?"

"I think we've got us a *bandido*, come down from the hill for a little taste."

The man began to glance about nervously, looking for a way out.

"Think this is worth waking Tanner for?" she asked.

"I think so," Sanchez said, still staring at the girl who was now staring back coyly.

"Well," Liz said, "go and do it!"

CHAPTER THIRTY-FOUR

When Tanner returned with Sanchez, Liz had the bandit dressed and waiting. To Sanchez's disappointment, she had also made the girl put her clothes on.

"You're not related to Katarina, are you?" Liz asked.

"No," the girl answered.

Liz looked at Tanner, and Tanner said, "Let her go."

The girl went home, and Liz, Tanner and Sanchez marched the bandit to the *cantina*. When they got there they all stood in front of the locked door and stared at each other.

"I guess I should have asked Katarina for a key," Liz said. "I'll go and get one."

"We'll wait here," Tanner said unnecessarily.

"What is it?" Katarina asked as she opened her

door. She had a robe on, but it was not fully closed at the top and Liz could see that the woman wore nothing underneath. Her hair was tousled and her lips seemed swollen. If Liz didn't know better she'd have sworn Katarina had a man in her bed.

"We've caught one of the bandits, Katarina. We'd like to use the *cantina* to question him."

"One of the bandits?"

"Yes. May I have a key for the *cantina*?"

"Yes, yes, of course," Katarina said. "Uh, come in. I will get it."

Liz stepped inside and closed the door.

"The key is in my bedroom," Katarina said.

Liz waited where she was while Katarina went to get the key. The door to the room was ajar and Liz could clearly hear Katarina talking to someone else. The other voice was also a woman's.

Katarina reappeared and handed Liz the key.

"I will get dressed and be there shortly."

"That's not necessary —"

"I want to see this man. I want to hear what he has to say."

"All right."

Liz hurried back to the *cantina* with the key.

They sat the bandit down at a table and formed a circle around him. Tanner, Sanchez, Liz, Brand and Northrop. The other two men had shown up while Liz was getting the key. Tate was still up on the roof on watch.

"Santos," Tanner said, "we want to know your

band's strength, and your plans. Do you plan to storm this town?''

Santos did not reply. Now that he had his clothes on, he was feeling much less vulnerable. For a moment Liz thought that perhaps they should strip him again.

They still weren't having much luck getting answers out of him by the time Katarina showed up.

''What has he told you?'' she demanded.

''Not much,'' Tanner said. He motioned Liz to step aside with him.

''What did you and Sanchez find out up there?''

She outlined for him what she had seen inside the tent, the ammunition and food stores that the bandits had. Then she told him that the best head count Sanchez could get put their strength at forty, easily.

''Forty,'' Tanner said, rubbing his jaw. ''Let's see what he has to say.''

''Tanner.''

''What?''

''I didn't see any sign of a cave.''

The look on Tanner's face was not a happy one, but he shrugged and said, ''You weren't looking for one.''

They walked back to where the bandit was sitting.

''Santos, we know that you have at least forty men up there and are well stocked in food and weapons.''

Santos looked at Tanner and smiled.

"If you think forty men is a lot, wait until the rest of our force gets here."

"The rest of your force?" Sanchez said.

"Our army," Santos responded, "for the revolution."

"Oh, great," Liz said. "We've got another bunch of bandits who think they're a revolutionary army."

"He's lying," Northrop said. "They don't have any more men coming."

Tanner took Santos' face in his hand, squeezing until the pain showed in the man's eyes.

"How about that, Santos?" he asked. "Are you a liar?"

"Wait and see."

"You will never see," Katarina said. Before anyone could react she produced a knife from the folds of her skirt and plunged it to the hilt in the man's chest. Santos had time for only a fleeting look of shock before he slumped over in his chair and died. They all stared at him in shock until he fell from the chair.

"Jesus Christ!" Tanner said. "What did you do that for?"

"They killed my father," she said. "I wanted to kill one of them."

"We could have gotten more information out of him."

"He would only have lied further," she said. "You got the information you were after, didn't you? From Elizabeth. You know how many men they have."

"At least forty."

"Can you fight such a force?"

Tanner wasn't so sure, but he said, "I think we can."

"How?"

"With the help of your people we can set up a good enough defense against an attack."

"And if that man was telling the truth?" Sanchez asked. "What if there are more men coming? Tanner, we can't handle much more than forty."

Tanner gave Sanchez a look that told him not to talk about it while Katarina was there.

"Come on, Katarina," Liz said, realizing it would be best if the Mexican girl left. "There is nothing else you can do tonight."

Katarina allowed Liz to lead her to the door.

"I will go back to bed, but tomorrow we will work with the women again, no?"

"Sure," Liz said. "We'll work them again."

Katarina looked back at the man on the floor and said, "I am glad I killed him."

Liz didn't know what to say to that, and Katarina left.

CHAPTER THIRTY-FIVE

Juan Dominguez entered the food and munitions tent and looked around for the canned peaches. Juan loved them because of the sweet nectar they were soaked in.

He did not find the case near the front of the tent, so he raised his storm lamp to look in the back. That was when he saw the man's foot. It looked as if it had been severed and left near the back of the tent. For a moment Juan almost lost his dinner. He moved closer and saw then that the foot was connected, but the rest of the body was outside the tent. Someone had cut a long opening in the back of the tent.

Juan rushed to the foot and stepped through the opening out of the tent.

"Antonio is dead," Jaime said. "Juan Dominguez found him behind the munitions tent."

Montalvo stood up from his bed and glowered at Jaime.

"How?"

"He was stabbed once, and then his throat was cut."

"Begin searching. Someone from that town is either up here, or has been up here. If they are still here I want them found."

"There is something else."

"What?"

"Santos is not in camp."

Montalvo knew that Santos had gone to see the girl from town, but he should have been back by now. Suddenly, Montalvo was short two men, and he didn't like it one bit.

He stepped forward, put his hand on Jaime's shoulder and pushed him toward the tent opening.

"Start the search! Hurry! I want the bastard found!"

Jaime left the tent and began shouting for men to start a search.

"What I'd like to do," Tanner said, "is bury some dynamite on both sides of the main street, with one of us at each end."

"As they ride into town we'd fire at the dynamite, exploding it," Tate said. He had been called down from the roof to sit in on the discussion.

"The problem with that is they'd see us doing it," Liz said. "Even at night we'd probably be visible because of the moonlight."

Tanner cursed the full moon.

"We can do it another way," Liz said.

"How?"

"We can put one of us at either end of the main street, each with one of the women."

"What does that accomplish?" Sanchez asked.

"We pick out the women with the strongest arms. They have to be able to throw a couple of sticks of dynamite across the street."

"And then we fire at it, exploding it," Tate said.

"Right."

"That'll work," Tanner said. "Good idea, Liz."

"Thanks."

"I have one modification," Tanner said. "If and when they come, they'll come from the north. I don't think they'll try to sneak up on us. I think we should put one person at the south end, and two at the north."

"Sounds good," Tate said.

"The rest of us will have to be scattered about, both on the roofs and inside the stores."

"We'll need extra weapons," Liz said, "and some of the women who can't shoot to reload for us."

"I want to help," Maria said. She had joined them, and had been quiet up until that point.

"Maria —" Tanner began.

"Chris, I want to help. I have a strong arm, I can throw the dynamite, or I can reload."

"I don't think we should discuss this —"

"You are trying to protect me as always, but what if we all die?" she asked. "I do not want to die hiding in a hotel room."

"All right, Maria," Tanner said, looking uncomfortable, "all right."

"When do you think they'll come?" Maria asked.

"We can't be sure —" Tanner began, but Liz cut him off.

"I think we can," Liz said. "I think they'll come tomorrow, or at least the day after."

"What makes you say that?"

"I didn't have a chance to tell you," she said, "but I had to kill one of their men."

"What happened?" Tate asked.

She quickly told them what had occurred.

"You did well to kill him without rousing the whole camp," Tate said.

"But I think she's right," Tanner said. "This is going to force them into making a move."

"Well, we'll just have to make sure we're ready for them," Liz said.

"This all sounds great," Northrop broke in, "but I'll ask again, what if the man wasn't lying?"

They all looked at the spot where Santos, the bandit, had been lying before they had dragged him out.

"If he wasn't lying," Tanner said, "we're going to be in a world of shit."

The bandits searched until daylight and found no one. They did, however, find signs that there had been people around their camp.

"This is a disgrace," Montalvo shouted. He had assembled his men in four lines and was pacing up and down in front of them. "We are spied on, one of our men is killed, and no one heard anything. A disgrace!''

There was a murmur of disapproval from the men. They did not like being shouted at, even by Montalvo.

"Silence!'' Montalvo yelled. ''If this revolution is to be successful I must have obedience.''

Grudgingly, the men fell silent.

''I want everyone to spend today tending to their weapons,'' Montalvo said. ''Tomorrow, we take the town.''

Now there was a murmur of approval.

''They will learn the folly of invading the camp of the next *presidente* of Mexico.''

The front line of men were sprayed with spittle from the mouth of the next *presidente* of Mexico, and so frightening was the look on the face of Montalvo that none of them dared wipe it away.

''Tomorrow,'' Montalvo said, ''their town, and their women, are ours.''

CHAPTER THIRTY-SIX

The next day was spent in preparation, everyone involved hoping that the bandits would not attack until they were ready for them.

Liz worked with the women who would be shooting, while Tanner — out of sight of the bandit lookout — was testing the other women to see who could throw a few sticks of dynamite the farthest. They didn't use real dynamite, but they'd managed to find some sticks that would weigh as much, and they'd tied them together. After that the women simply stepped up to a line and let fly, with Sanchez judging the distance.

Brand, Northrop and Tate went about the town picking out the best spots for guns to be placed. Tate checked out the rooftops, while Brand chose the storefronts and Northrop selected alleys and other possibilities.

Almost everyone was busy, and it did not escape the notice of the bandit scout. The only people he couldn't see were the women who were working with Tanner.

"What are they doing?" Jaime asked the lookout, a man called Anselmo.

The lookout laughed and said, "They are running around like chickens without heads. I think they have been driven mad by fear."

Jaime doubted that. Anyone who had the nerve to sneak into their camp at night would certainly not go mad from fear. More than likely they were readying the town to meet the charge of Montalvo's army.

Suddenly, Jaime had an idea. Whatever the people from the town could do, he could do better.

He was going to town.

"All right, that's enough," Tanner called out. "Thank you for coming, ladies. Sanchez, take the rest of them and start showing them how to load."

"Right."

The three women Tanner chose to throw the dynamite were Maria, Nina, the liverygirl who had been caught with the bandit, and a handsome woman in her early forties named Rosa.

Tanner had already decided that he would put Maria at the south end of town, where there would be no danger. Of course, in the event that they were overrun, it wouldn't make much difference where she was, but maybe the bandits would leave her alive.

Or would that be worse than dying, he wondered.

Since it was light out and he was going *down* not *up*, Jaime made much better time than Liz and Sanchez had the night before.

Everyone in town was so busy that none of them saw him make his way to the back of a building and climb to the roof. He easily eluded the eyes of the lookout, a woman who had been instructed to watch for a large force.

Peering over the edge of the roof Jaime saw a figure leaning against the ledge on the other side, but there was something odd about the figure. It didn't move, and it was shaped funny. There was one other little matter.

It had a hat on, but it had no head.

As quietly as he came, Jaime left, feeling very satisfied with himself.

Late in the afternoon Tanner told everyone to take a break, and he and his people went to the *cantina*.

He took a report from each of them.

Tate had picked out the rooftops with the best vantage points, while Brand had chosen the stores with the best view of the streets. Northrop had found some spots where they could build barricades.

"All right," Tanner said, "Tate, you'll set the

people up on the rooftops. It'll have to be Sanchez, Brand and Northrop. I want you and Liz free to move around and help the women.''

''I'll show them the rooftops I picked after lunch.''

''Fine. Liz?''

''The women are as ready as they'll ever be. I've instructed them as to who will get rifles and who will get shotguns.''

''Good. Sanchez?''

''I've got the women practicing loading. They'll be fine.''

''All right. I think that does it.''

''Where do I go?'' Maria said.

''Tate will show you, Maria.''

She nodded, knowing Tanner would tell Tate where to put her.

''And you?'' Liz asked.

''I'll take one of the barricades, close to the street. If I get a chance, I want to try and kill their leader. I'll have to be close to pick him out.''

Vita and Lily brought beers for everyone and promised that lunch would soon follow.

''After lunch I think we should start taking turns on watch. That'll be better than using inexperienced women,'' Tanner said. ''We'll work out a schedule.''

The others nodded, and while they waited for lunch they fell into a pensive, awkward silence. No one knew what to say to break it.

CHAPTER THIRTY-SEVEN

"Dummies?" Montalvo said.

"Dummies," Jaime repeated. "All of the men on the rooftops are dummies."

Montalvo began to laugh.

"They have no men?" he said incredulously. "It is a town of women."

"Except for the five men who rode into town," Jaime told him. "They are obviously hired guns who are trying to help the town resist us."

"Women," Montalvo said, his tone one of awe. He looked at Jaime and said, "We will go in tomorrow, Jaime. In the morning."

"Don't you think we should wait for the rest of our men?" Jaime asked. "A show of force might prevent —"

"A show of force to women?" Montalvo said. "And five men? No, my friend, we will go in tomorrow. We will take their guns away from them and chastize them severely for resisting us, and then we will have our revolution headquarters."

"Hector —"

"And I have a truly wonderful idea," Montalvo said. "You, Jaime, will go down and tell them we are coming."

"Warn them?"

"Tell them," Montalvo said, "so that they may make their peace with God."

"Hector —"

"Go, Jaime. Do as I say. Do not let it be said that *presidente* Montalvo is not a benevolent leader."

Liz and Tate set up the schedule of watches through the night. The rest of the day would be spent in preparation for the actual attack.

Liz and Tanner were working on the barricade that Tanner would use when Tate, who was on watch, shouted, "Rider coming in!"

Liz and Tanner stood up and drew their guns until the rider came into view. They saw the rider look up to the rooftop where Tate was, so he knew he was covered. They stepped out into the street to meet him. Some of the women who were working stopped and lined the street on each side, wanting to hear what was going to be said.

"That's far enough," Tanner warned.

Liz thought that this was probably one of the ugliest men she'd ever seen. He was short and squat, with thinning hair and a bulbous nose. He wore twin *bandoliers* across his chest, which was almost the official badge of the *bandido*.

"I come with a message."

"From your leader?" Tanner said.

"From the next *presidente* of Mexico, Hector Enrique Montalvo."

"Oh, brother," Liz said beneath her breath.

"He wishes for you to have this night to make your peace with God. Tomorrow, we come to take the town."

"Not without a fight."

The man grinned, revealing yellow teeth.

"With dummies?" he asked.

"With guns," Liz said.

The man looked directly at her and said, "Guns held by women." He looked at Tanner and said, "You and your men will be killed. So will any women who resist. The rest will be allowed to live. Make your peace."

The rider turned his horse and began to ride out. Tanner was tempted to send the bandits a message by shooting the messenger in the back, but he decided to let the man go.

"Make our peace," Liz repeated.

"You know," Tanner said, low enough for only Liz to hear him, "I'm starting to think that taking this job might not have been such a good idea."

CHAPTER THIRTY-EIGHT

Tanner was indeed sorry he had taken this job. As he lay in bed with Maria that night he knew that he'd been foolish. As much as Maria meant to him, he knew he'd made an error by allowing a woman to get to him after all these years. He'd taken this job because he was greedy and had minimized the risks to himself, and to the others.

Now he just might be responsible not only for his death, but for all their deaths.

How do you make peace with God with that hanging over your head?

CHAPTER THIRTY-NINE

They were all up before first light and in place.

Northrop and Maria were on a roof south of town. To Northrop it was a waste of time. The bandits had announced that they were coming; why would they try to sneak in the back way? Once the action started, he had decided, he was hauling ass to the north end of town.

The two northern rooftops, across from each other, were manned — and womanned — by Sanchez and Brand, each with one of the women Tanner had chosen.

Tanner was positioned behind his barricade, which was made of wood from broken, piled up furniture and torn up floorboards.

Tate was in a storefront with a woman to reload his guns. He had set up teams of women in similar storefronts, one to shoot and one to reload.

Liz was across the street in a like situation. She knew that Katarina was standing at the door of the *cantina* with a gun, ready to kill some more of the bandits she was sure were responsible for her father's death.

Liz wondered idly if they'd ever know for sure who killed Mendez, or if the shootout they'd had in Mexico City was at all involved with this.

There were enough weapons in town so that almost all of them had two guns each, one to fire while the other was being reloaded.

Now all they had to do was wait.

Montalvo came down off the ridge with thirty-seven men, fully expecting to simply ride into town and take it over.

He was in for a rude surprise.

"Here they come!" Sanchez shouted.

They all watched while the bandits rode to the edge of town and stopped. Once again the ugly messenger from the day before was dispatched forward. He rode to a point where he could easily be heard.

"If you will throw down your weapons now," he shouted, "your lives will be spared. You will be permitted to serve the next *presidente* —"

Katarina stepped out of the *cantina*, shouted, "Never!" and fired once. The messenger was struck in the chest by the bullet and knocked off his horse.

Well, Liz thought, at least she was telling the truth about being able to shoot.

Jaime Santana lay on the ground, a burning pain in

his chest. It wasn't fair, he thought. Hector was the one who should have been shot.

This was all Hector's fault.

"Shit!" Tanner said. "I wish she hadn't done that."

Hector watched Jaime fall from his horse.

"I gave them a chance," he said to no one in particular. He raised his hand, and signaled his "army" to attack.

The first two attacks were a blur.

The women who were throwing the dynamite did a fine job. They threw two sticks tied together into the midst of the charging bandits, and Sanchez and Brand were on the mark, hitting them with either their first or second shot. The ensuing explosions scattered the bandits, killed more than a few, and drove them back twice.

The second time they retreated from sight in order to regroup. This gave the people in the town time to take stock of their own damages.

Liz and Tate came out and Tanner went to meet them.

"What's our damage?" Tanner asked.

Liz sent a couple of the women to find out if anyone was hurt.

"What do you think?" Tate asked Tanner.

"Oh, they'll be back. We made a lot of noise, but I only see about ten or twelve bodies."

"Part of the problem is that the dynamite scatters them," Liz said. "The women with rifles aren't hitting the mark. If they fire when the bandits are bunched, they'll hit more."

"Yeah, but will they kill more than we're killing with the dynamite?" Tanner asked.

"Probably not."

"We'll keep using the dynamite."

The women returned and reported that there were very few injuries, and what there were were minor.

"Well, we haven't given them much of a chance to mount an offensive," Tanner said.

"Let's keep it that way," Liz said.

"I haven't been able to spot the leader," Tanner complained. "I think he's staying back —"

"Coming back!" Sanchez shouted.

They were closer to Tate's storefront than Liz's, so they both headed for there and Tanner went back to his barricade.

This time when they attacked they came in scattered, so that the dynamite, when it exploded, did less damage. Staying scattered also reduced the effectiveness of the women who were firing.

Liz, Tate and Tanner were doing most of the damage, but this time the bandits *were* able to mount an offensive, firing into the storefronts, shattering windows and sending shards of glass inside.

Liz and Tate fell back when their window shattered, some of the glass cutting their hands and faces. A woman next to Liz caught a sharp shard of glass in the throat and fell over, gagging on her own blood.

A few of the bandits had been instructed to pick off the men on the rooftops who were doing the damage with the dynamite. Sanchez and Brand leapt back as a hail of bullets fell on them, but the women who were helping them were not as quick. Both were hit several times, and died quickly.

When the bandits pulled back again, Liz, Tate and Tanner again took stock.

"Worse this time," Liz said. "We've got four dead women, several others seriously injured."

"And we killed less of them this time," Tanner said. "They've gotten smart, and that's not good for us."

"Comin' back!" Brand shouted.

"And they're taking less time between attacks," Tate shouted as they all scrambled for their positions.

This time Sanchez and Brand had to toss their own dynamite, making the explosions fewer and even less effective.

Northrop stood it as long as he could, holding his position south of town, until finally he couldn't take it any longer.

"This is bullshit," he said to Maria, and left his position.

Maria, unsure about what to do, followed, holding dynamite in each hand.

When the next attack came it caught both Northrop and Maria in the middle of the street.

Liz saw Maria and shouted, "Go back!" but her words were lost in the noise of the shooting.

Northrop was hit almost immediately, a bullet striking him in the left shoulder, spinning him around and knocking him to the ground. Maria froze in the center of the street, and a random bullet managed to strike one of the sticks of dynamite she held in her hand.

Liz watched as Maria was literally blown to pieces.

"Jesus," she said.

"Keep firing!" Tate yelled.

Sanchez was standing to toss some dynamite when a bullet took off the top of his head.

Katarina stepped out of the *cantina* in order to get a better shot, and a bullet buried itself between her breasts.

Northrop began to crawl, trying to get out of the street, and two bandits simply ran him down with their horses. Tate killed one of them, and Liz the other.

When the bandits withdrew this time, the town's defenses were in tatters.

CHAPTER FORTY

Liz and Tate, both bleeding from cuts on their hands and faces, joined Tanner at his barricade.

"How we doing?" Tanner asked.

"It's bad," Liz said. "Both Northrop and Sanchez are dead."

"Northrop? What about Maria?"

Liz hesitated a split second, then said, "I haven't seen her."

"What about the women?"

"Three more dead," Liz said, "including Katarina."

"I'm starting to think it may be time to pull out," Tanner said.

"How?" Liz asked.

"The south end of town."

"I think Liz means how can we pull out and

leave these people to the mercy of the bandits,'' Tate said.

"Maybe after we leave, the bandits will leave them alone.''

They all stopped talking at that point because they expected to hear Brand calling out that the bandits were coming back. But he didn't. The town was almost completely silent.

"They're taking a longer break this time,'' Tanner said.

"Probably want to make us stop and think,'' Tate said.

"They're succeeding,'' Liz muttered.

A man named Ricardo came down from the ridge and found Montalvo.

"Jefe," he said, "the others have arrived.''

"Excellent,'' Montalvo said. "They have put up a valiant fight, but now we have them. Ricardo, instruct half of our men to circle the town and come in from the south.''

"Here they come!'' Brand shouted. "Jesus Christ, there's more of them!''

The bandits approached slowly, and Liz saw that their number had suddenly doubled.

"Well, I guess Santos wasn't lying,'' she said.

Tate turned to agree with her and saw more men approaching from the south end.

"He sure wasn't,'' he said. "Tanner, we've got to get off the street and find some cover. Come on!''

He pulled Tanner by the arm and the three of

them scrambled back to a storefront just before the bandits launched their attack.

Suddenly, the street was filled with bandits, all firing at the rooftops and into the storefronts.

From the roof Brand threw his last sticks of dynamite, but before he could fire on them he was hit in the chest. He staggered backward, tried to compensate by throwing his weight forward, and succeeded in throwing himself off the roof.

The din was deafening and Liz couldn't hear what Tate was shouting into her ear. She just kept firing, and reloading. The women who had been reloading for them were either dead or hiding.

Liz, Tate and Tanner were in the general store. There had been such a barrage of lead that every item that had been on shelves was now on the floor. Most of the shelves themselves had been chewed to pieces.

Suddenly Tanner lurched to his feet and said, "I've got to find Maria."

"You'll be hit!" Tate shouted, but Liz saw that Tanner had already been hit. He was bleeding from the shoulder, and as he got to his feet to climb out through the broken window another bullet hit him in the side. He fell back against Tate, knocking him to the floor. Liz turned to see if Tate had been hit, and felt something tug at her left sleeve.

Suddenly, it was quiet.

Tate struggled off the floor and saw the blood on Liz's sleeve.

"You're wounded!" he said.

"It's just a nick. Let's see what's happening out there."

They looked outside and saw the street was empty. There were several bodies left behind, but the town's defenses had certainly done no major damage to the reinforced bandit horde.

"How's Tanner?" Liz asked.

"He's done."

"That leaves you, me and the women," Liz said.

"However many are left."

"Listen . . ."

She could hear horses, but they were moving slowly.

They watched as five men rode into the center of the street. Four of them flanked the fifth, protecting him with their bodies.

"The leader," Liz said.

"We could probably pick him off," Tate said, "but it wouldn't stop them. Let's hear what he has to say."

"Hombres!" the leader shouted. "The women may throw down their weapons and come out."

Tate shouted back, "What about us?"

"Most of you are dead," he said. "The rest of you will be executed."

"Do you think he'd talk a deal?" Liz asked.

In spite of himself, Tate laughed.

The leader spoke now in rapid Spanish, and Liz thought she caught the gist of it.

"I think he's telling the women to throw down their guns and come out."

"If they do it," Tate said, "that really leaves the two of us."

Liz and Tate watched and then, slowly, women came out of the shattered storefronts. They walked up to the leader, who spoke to them. Then they went to the *cantina*.

"He's herding them into the *cantina*," Liz said. "Do you think he's going to kill them?"

"No," Tate said. "I think he's going to kill us."

Liz picked up Tanner's gun, ejected the spent shells and reloaded. Tate also had two guns in his hands.

"I have an idea, if you're interested," Tate said.

"What?"

"You're a woman. Maybe he'll let you go out with the others."

"I'm not from the town," she said, "and I don't have time to change my hair color to try and blend in. Let's just drop it, okay?"

"Liz?"

"I'm not going out."

"Okay, it was just an idea."

"A piss poor one," she said.

Tate leaned over and they kissed.

"Señor?" the leader shouted.

"Yeah!" Tate answered.

"All of the women have come out. Some of them are dead, but most of them have survived."

"For how long?"

"I will not kill them, señor. That was not my goal. My goal was to take this town, and now I have it."

"I guess you're pretty satisfied, then!" Tate shouted.

"I will be, as soon as you are dead. How many of you are left?"

"There's two of us!" Liz shouted before Tate could open his mouth.

"Ah, the blonde-haired woman?"

"That's right," she said.

"Let her go . . ." Tate groped for the man's

name, which the messenger had given, and found it. "Let her go, Montalvo."

"She is a mercenary, señor, as are you. I cannot let her go. I must show these women the folly of their ways."

"Get it over with, then."

"Come out so you can be executed with dignity."

"Come in and get us," Liz said.

"Tough talk," Tate said to her, and she showed him her tongue.

Montalvo made a waving motion and gradually the street filled up with bandits.

"He looks like he's got a pretty big army," Liz said. "How do you think they'll do in Mexico City?"

"They'll chew him up and spit him out."

"I wish I could see that," Liz said.

"Me, too."

There was a loud sound then, and it took a moment for Liz and Tate to identify it. It was the sound of all those guns being cocked.

"Señor, señorita, are you coming out?"

"Wait a minute," Liz said to Tate. She took her orange neckerchief out of her pocket, where it had been forgotten all this time. She put it on and knotted it, then saw Tate looking at her.

"Maybe after this," she said, "we will reach mythic proportions."

He smiled at her and said, "Ready, Angel Eyes?"

"Ready."

They cocked their guns and shouted, "We're coming out!"